MW00833812

Print ISBN: 978-1-958890-53-0
Ebook ISBN: 979-8-88531-555-5

Published by BookLocker.com, Inc., Trenton, Georgia.

This is a work of historical fiction, based on actual persons and events. The author has taken creative liberty with many details to enhance the reader's experience.

BookLocker.com, Inc.

Edition

Library of Congress Cataloguing in Publication Data
Davis, Dadriene
The Culture by Dadriene Davis
Library of Congress Control Number: 2023914283

# Four The Culture

Dadriene Davis

BookLocker
Trenton, Georgia

To my cousin, Kwalei Reynolds,
You had a heart of gold that inspired me to pursue my dreams no matter what I endured in life. Thank you for teaching me to stay strong! Fly high, Kwa!
I love you always.

       - Dadriene

# Table of Contents

# Prologue

Summer in the South was always an interesting experience. This was during a time when many children were required to work starting around the tender ages of four and five. Many of them would be out in the fields, picking cotton and tobacco for maybe twenty dollars a day. Many African American households had big families, especially in the more rural areas. Ten children to one house was normal, and every child was put to work during the hot summer to save money for the winter months.

That twenty dollars would add up.

Ezell Blair was a boy from the city. The city of Greensboro that is. He knew nothing of laboring in a cotton field. In fact, he was not aware that cotton fields existed in North Carolina after slavery was abolished. He was a fourteen-year-old kid who delivered newspapers from one doorstep to the next. He loved his job, and he did it well with a smile that could brighten anyone's day. The segregated South was an unreal place to live, even though it was *terribly* real. The further you went down South, the more you would understand its atrocities.

It was a hot summer night in August of 1955 in the Mississippi Delta. Every creature near the Tallahatchie River could be heard sounding off through the starry, black sky. The sound was melodic. The sound of nature. Birds and crickets chirping over the flowing water. The sound of a child screaming.

The sound of a child screaming...

In a nearby barn, there was a wail that could have woken a city, if the location was not as secluded as it was. Several wails followed as a young boy, maybe in his early teen years, scrambled through the dirt in the shed, his mouth flooded with blood. He was cornered by two adult men. One of them had been assaulting the boy with the butt of a gun. He used every swear word and slur he could think of as he continued the attack, kicking the boy in the stomach. "This how your kind treat women in Chicago?" he demanded. "I'm sick of y'all coming down here, startin' trouble!"

The child could hardly respond. Apart from his bleeding mouth and several missing teeth, he also stuttered tremendously as he tried to plead his case. "I—I didn't do it!" he cried.

His words fell on deaf ears. One of the guys, who appeared to be quite younger than the other, had rolled in a cotton gin fan. The older man's eyes held no remorse as he turned the gun directly toward the quivering boy. This was the end. Neither one of the men would regret this moment. Ever.

"We'll make an example out of you."

*"Very truly I tell you, unless a kernel of wheat falls to the ground and dies, it remains only a single seed. But if it dies, it produces many seeds." John 12:24*

# Chapter One:
# The Blair Legacy

Ezell examined himself in the bathroom mirror. He was not tall by any measure. His physical selling point was his infectious smile. He could not help but show all whites in the reflection looking back at him, of a boy almost through puberty. Ezell had now reached sixteen years of age. He took pride in the few chin hairs he had likely grown over the last year. The young man flexed his muscles before the headline of a newspaper caught his attention from a stand in the corner.

He picked up the paper. *Nation Shocked by Lynching of Chicago Youth.* Ezell's eyes grew dull as they scanned the paper. It soon became clear he had read the article at least a dozen times but had not registered the events that unfolded in Money, Mississippi. Maybe he would have needed to be there to understand. He was the same age as Emmett Till, the child slaughtered by two white men a few years prior for allegedly whistling at one of their wives. The horrors of this event shook the world and reminded the United States of what life was like in the South. Furthermore, it reminded Ezell of the consequences he could face if he stepped out of line. This was too much to take in.

Ezell placed the newspaper back on the stand. He cleared his throat and began to hum. The hum flowed into a song. "You Send Me" was a song he loved by Sam Cooke. He sang to his reflection as if he were practicing to charm someone else. The solo rehearsal was interrupted by a few loud thuds on the door. "Junior, hurry up!" Ezell was not an only child. He had two younger sisters, Jean and Sheila. Jean was only eight months younger than he was. She had been born prematurely and was not expected to survive infancy, but my God, was she here.

"Junior, I need my tweezers!" the girl yelled. "You're gonna make us all late!" Ezell sighed as his sister banged on the door repeatedly. It was not that serious. He opened the door.

"Yes, Jean?" he said, nonchalantly.

Jean rushed past her brother. "You know we've only got one bathroom," she said. "I should've known you were in here fantasizing about... whoever."

Ezell leaned against the sink as his sister retrieved the tweezers from the stand. "Is Dad up yet?" he asked, quietly.

Jean began plucking her eyebrows in the mirror. "Yes, and you know he's on a tight schedule, so please don't take all day to get ready."

Ezell lowered his voice into a whisper. "Well, I talked to him about the competition."

Jean shook her head. "Yeah, I know, but I wouldn't get my hopes up if I were you, Junior," she replied.

"Have some faith." Ezell grunted. "He said he'd think about it."

Jean sighed. "Yeah, but I can't witness another blow up between you two," she whispered while adjusting her glasses. "He wants us to focus on school. That's all you need to be worried about right now."

Jean made her exit while Ezell took one final observation of himself in the mirror. He may not have been completely satisfied with himself, but no one had to know that. No one ever questioned if he was insecure in any way. Ezell was known for his sheer charisma, a trait he flaunted to its full capacity.

As a child, he'd owned a Jerry Mahoney doll and would put on puppet shows to entertain anyone who would watch. Now as a teenager he still owned the exact same doll and, if asked, he would put on a puppet show to entertain anyone who would watch. The doll sat on the dresser in his room next to a record player. There were records stacked on top of one another—all different artists and genres. Chuck Berry was the most popular black artist out, and Ezell had mastered the musician's iconic duck walk, usually using a broom in place of a guitar.

After he was dressed, he made his way to the kitchen. His mother was heating a hot comb she would use to style Sheila's hair. Mrs. Corine lifted the comb from the eye of the stove, slightly distracted by the news on the television. Nine children in Little Rock, Arkansas were being escorted into a high school by the National Guard in an attempt to desegregate the school. "Lord, those are some brave children," she said while gesturing at Sheila. The youngest daughter of the Blair family had been eating cereal at the table across from her grandmother, Adelia. The elderly woman was sewing a quilt, fully engaged in the events unfolding in Arkansas.

Jean paid no attention to the television as she entered the kitchen. "Mama, have you seen my compact?" she asked.

Corine pointed toward part of the counter where a compact mirror sat next to a radio. Jean picked up the item before placing her ear closer to the soft music. Any song by Little Richard was perfect to start the day off with. "Mama, it's our song!" she shouted.

Corine tried not to break her focus as she curled Sheila's hair. "I can't hear it."

Adelia was thankful the news report had finished just in time, because Jean turned the speaker's knob all the way until it stopped. The kitchen was now full of the sound of rock and roll. Jean used a hairbrush she probably should not have carried into the kitchen as a microphone and began singing to her grandmother at the table.

Ezell entered the kitchen, amused by Sheila's hairstyle just as he was every morning. Corine would always leave a dent in the bang she curled over her daughter's forehead that irritated the child so much she could not wait to be older and do her own hair. But at that moment, Sheila was performing with her mother and sister, using the hot comb for the same reason Jean had the hairbrush. Ezell tried to ignore the concert, hugging his grandmother before taking an orange from a dish on the table. "What happened to us being on a tight schedule?" he asked Jean with an unserious look on his face.

Jean ignored the question, turning to take a wooden spoon from the drawer next to her. Ezell placed the orange on the counter to prepare himself. He caught the spoon and began his comeback tour as an international singer. Internationally in his family's kitchen. It did not matter one bit. As soon as he caught the makeshift microphone, he was a world-renowned artist and performed as such. His mother, grandmother, and sisters gleamed as the young boy sang along with Little Richard. It had been a long time since he bonded with his family through music, though it was a known fact that Ezell was a music lover. He could demand any audience's attention on any stage if given the opportunity. Ezell was used to being the center of attention, being the only boy, so the spotlight was nothing new to him. Then, just before the grand finale—

*Click.*

The children had barely broken a sweat when the music came to an abrupt stop. They turned to see Ezell Sr. standing next to the radio in a trench coat with a briefcase in one hand. Their father had a menacing presence about him. He was not the most approachable person and clearly not someone you wanted to have waiting on you, because Ezell quickly placed the spoon on the kitchen table, then positioned himself as if he were a cadet in basic training. "Morning, Dad..." he whimpered.

"I told you to be ready when I walked out the door," the man said. At times, his voice could be more intimidating than his presence was. "Yet you're here, wasting time."

Ezell took a deep breath. "I'm dressed, Dad. I'm ready to go," he said. "Well, actually, I need to grab my jacket."

Ezell Sr. shook his head as his son rushed past him. "You would've had time to grab your jacket if you weren't in here singin' and carryin' on." He turned to give Corine a kiss on the cheek as Jean rolled her eyes and headed toward the hall.

\*

Ezell entered the living room with a briefcase. Like father, like son. He straightened his fedora hat as a car horn blew from the driveway. "Junior, let's tighten up!" he heard his father yell. Then on the table something caught his attention. Ezell picked up a piece of paper laying atop of other papers. Geography questions... and answers. He peered around the room. No one was watching. No one was present but himself, so he plunged the paper into his briefcase amid several more car horns and the sound of his impatient father's voice.

Both of Ezell's parents were schoolteachers. Fortunately, but most times unfortunately, Ezell Sr. taught at Dudley High School where both Ezell and Jean attended. He was also Ezell's geography teacher. Though Ezell Sr. was a tough man, a trait likely instilled in him after fighting in World War II, he was a hands-on father who played an active role in the life choices of his children. He and his wife had both attended North Carolina Agricultural and Technical University in Greensboro, North Carolina, and for Ezell Sr., his children carrying on the family's legacy at the institution was not up for debate. Ezell would sometimes admit to himself that he was a handful and would subtly defy his father's orders, especially about matters concerning his own future. Yes, college was an option for Ezell, but during that time in his life other things piqued his interest even more.

\*

Maybe it was her hair. Her smile. The way she carried herself with so much elegance and grace. Ezell grinned from ear to ear as one of his female classmates returned the shabby slide rule he let her borrow in precalculus. She was *the one*. This was who he wanted to spend the rest of his life with. But first, he had to acknowledge the young lady he would often loan his coat to in their frigid world history class. She was the epitome of wife material.

"Hi, E.Z.," a cheerleader greeted Ezell as he made his way down the hallway. He turned one eighty, stumbling over his words.

"Hi," the enamored boy stuttered with glistening eyes. It was love at first sight. This was the moment he had dreamed of. The random girl he had only seen around school a few times went out of her way to speak to him... *first*. Ezell had found his other half.

The lovestruck teenager turned into the gentlemen's bathroom where three other guys waited for him. Willie, Thurman, and John were Ezell's bandmates. The four of them had formed a quartet earlier that year and would often rehearse in the restroom during class transitions for a few minutes, which was really all the time they had. As soon as Ezell entered, John, who was the baritone of the group, started the song. John's voice was used to mimic a bass guitar while the other three members provided the vocals. Ezell had a warm tenor voice, and during the bridge of the song he transitioned to falsetto, holding out several lengthy notes as his bandmates *doo wopped* next to him.

At that time, quartets were very popular. If you could sing, it was common to connect with others who could do so as well, and the rest was history. Many music groups would enter local competitions in hopes of becoming the next big thing. Singing was not necessarily a *manly* talent, but the guys who could do it were not ashamed of their gift, especially since it could be used to woo women. That was Ezell's motive anyway. He could hardly focus on the solo part as his bright eyes wandered across the ceiling.

The other three members stopped singing. "E.Z., what's gotten into you?" Willie demanded. "We haven't got all day to rehearse the song."

Ezell broke out of his trance. "I'm sorry, fellas," he said. "What part were we on again?"

John groaned. "See, if you put as much focus into music as you do on your search for a soulmate, we might actually sound like something."

Thurman nodded. "This is the same reason you can't pull it together on the track field either."

Ezell had nearly forgotten he was also an athlete. *Who cares?*

"Listen, I don't need you all to worry about me," he replied. "We need to be concerned about New Farmers of

America. We've got a good chance of winning since we already beat out those guys from Raleigh."

Willie digressed. "Ezell, you're being so positive about this whole competition, but you're forgetting one thing—you're the only one who hasn't paid your end of the money we need to enter."

Ezell looked into the eyes of his bandmates. They had clearly discussed this matter before he arrived. Now they were waiting to hear the decision. *Was E.Z. in or out?*

Ezell felt cornered. "Why would I not pay my end?" he asked in a tone that suggested he knew the answer to his own question.

"C'mon, E.Z., you know your dad doesn't commend you singing," John stated the obvious. "Especially in a competition where everyone would know you're his son."

Ezell looked away from them as if he had been stung by the tail of a scorpion. The truth hurt, but it was important to be optimistic anyway. "Relax, guys," he began his reassurance, "my dad just has to take care of a few things around the house and then he's gonna pay my way in. Let's focus on what we need to do here."

The other singers shrugged. *Sounds like a plan.* Who was to say what Ezell's father would or would not do? They needed to rehearse either way. Even with the competition being several months out, practice made perfect, and Ezell always strived for perfection.

He had no choice—his family had high expectations for him. Ezell Sr. was a crafty man. He and Ezell had built the house their family lived in. He had hopes of his son using his inherited abilities of fine architecture and taking on a major of engineering at his alma mater, A&T. Therefore, Ezell was never vocal about his own goals, knowing that his father would not approve.

So, at that point, it was easier not to challenge authority and just go with the flow—a natural mentality for Ezell Blair Jr.

# Chapter Two:
# Manchild

Chemistry class was a bore. It was obvious that most children only took these advanced courses because it looked good on a transcript for college applications. Many of them stared blankly at their instructor as she lectured them on chemical reactions. Ezell sat at the back of the class next to David Richmond. They laughed, not focused on the subject being discussed. No one else was really paying attention to the teacher either. No one but Franklin McCain.

Franklin sat at a table in the front row—a personal decision deemed inconsiderate for those around him given his size. Franklin stood around 6'2 or 6'3. He could have easily been a linebacker for the football team, but instead of taking on sports as he was normally encouraged to, he kept his head in the books. Franklin would answer every question in class if the teacher would allow him to. Again, due to his unmissable physique, the teacher could never pretend not to see his hand raised, no matter how much she wanted someone else to answer a question.

There were, however, two students at the back of the class who could not even pretend to be interested in the lecture. Instead, Ezell and David were doodling in the raggedy, hand-me-down textbooks they were given, creating vulgar pictures the next owners would likely laugh at. The teacher called out to them. "Mr. Blair, Mr.

Richmond. Would you please tell me the definition of a catalyst?"

Ezell panicked. The old *"Let's see if you were paying attention"* trick was so outdated, and yet there they were. All eyes on the two of them. Ezell did love the spotlight, but not under those circumstances. "Uh," he tried to sound sure of himself while automatically turning the page of the textbook, hoping the definition would be somewhere close by. "A catalyst... a catalyst—" he stuttered.

"A catalyst is any substance that can increase the rate of a reaction without itself being consumed." David's eyes had not looked away from the teacher since she put them on the spot, and yet somehow, he stated the definition as if he had rehearsed it for, well, *class*. The teacher could have been embarrassed, but surprisingly, she seemed rather impressed at her student's sharp intellect and readiness.

David bumped knuckles with Ezell as the class continued with the lesson. Ezell never knew how his friend did it. How David could do so many things at once was always a mystery. He was a stellar student and athlete. In fact, David had just become a legend at Dudley High, claiming the champion title in the state's national high jump event.

David was the closest thing to a superhero Ezell thought he would ever know. At every track meet, he would stand on the sidelines, encouraging the gifted sportsman to do his best. Ezell pushed himself harder while watching his friend quite literally rise above the bar set for him.

There were no limits for the high jump champ. *David can do anything.*

\*

Ezell could never stay seated during lunch time. He always felt the need to interact with everyone around him, especially the women who could potentially be his true love. Yes, Ezell was a proud, hopeless romantic. Despite his unmistakable charm, it was not rare for the women he showed interest in to take interest in another guy. A bigger, taller guy, like David and Franklin.

David was having a disagreement with his girlfriend at the table he sat at. Franklin sat across from the bickering couple, trying to be invisible. The frustrated woman was curious as to what David's plans would be after they graduated high school. "So, do you plan to go to college?" she inquired. "Can you be a student and hold down a job at the same time?"

David waited to respond. Truthfully, he was not entirely sure. Despite being an exceptional student, athlete, and school president, David was still a teenager trying to find his way in the world. "I'll figure it out," he said calmly, attempting to end the series of questions. It did not work.

"But David, how long will it take you to figure it out?!" His girlfriend was desperate for an answer now, but David was ready to enjoy the meal before him. David loved to eat.

"We can talk about this later," he said in a sterner tone. The girl knew he meant business. The debate was over. She grabbed her books and purse, preparing to leave the argument at the table.

"Well, I'm proud of everything you've accomplished so far, Mr. High Jump Champ," she said. "I'll see ya around."

David felt bad he'd ended the conversation in that manner but relieved he could finally eat in peace. Ezell was glad he could finally take his seat at the table now that things had cooled down. "Wouldn't be a normal day if you weren't mingling with every girl out here, E.Z.," Franklin said.

Ezell laughed. "I just want to be like David," he replied. "There's plenty of fish out there, may as well try as many as you can, ain't that right, Hoppergrass?" This was the nickname they had given David because his legs would allow him to leap vigorously into the air just like the insect can.

David shook his head. "That's *your* motto, not mine, and I wish y'all would stop calling me that."

Franklin chuckled. "But you earned it, *high jump champ*."

David ignored the comment. "When does your train leave for D.C., Frank?"

Ezell peered at Franklin. "You're heading back to D.C. already?"

Franklin nodded. "Can you believe the school year is almost over? I-"

Ezell never waited for people to complete a sentence before he bombarded them with more questions. "What are you gonna do when you get back?!" he asked with genuine excitement and curiosity.

Franklin, unlike many of his peers, had his entire life planned out, and there was nothing in this world that would cause him to deviate from achieving his goals, a trait that was inspiring to Ezell. "Well, I'm gonna finish my senior year up North, then I'm coming back down South for college."

Ezell and David glanced at each other. "What school are you applying to?" Ezell asked.

"A&T," Franklin said, gleefully, "right here in Greensboro. It's one of the best schools to study biology."

David was baffled by the statement. "But aren't the schools up North more... advanced?" he asked.

Franklin took a small breath. "Better schools don't mean better treatment for people like us," he replied. "I believe a predominantly black college suits me better. The point of me coming to live here for a school year was to get in-state tuition at A&T."

The North Carolina native had grown up in Washington D.C. for most of his life. Southerners would often assume that because the North was mostly integrated that it made life far easier than the racially divided South, but Franklin knew better.

David shared his sentiments. "I think that was a smart decision. I've been looking at A&T for some time now. It's a nice campus."

Franklin tried to hide the excitement in his eyes, removing his glasses and pretending to clean them. "Yeah, man, we should all go," he said, wiping the clear lenses with the tail of his polo shirt. "I haven't made too many friends down here, and it's always good to have people you know around when you're in unfamiliar territory."

The comment did not surprise Ezell. Though Franklin was immensely driven and goal-oriented, he was also a family guy who considered true companionship a success right along with his other endeavors. Ezell was not convinced, however. "I'm not going to A&T," he said. "Both of my parents went there, and I don't want to live in my dad's shadow forever."

Franklin was inquisitive. "Then where are you going?"

David could not wait to answer for Ezell. "He wants to go to Lincoln College in Illinois," he said with an evil smirk on his face, "as if his dad is gonna let that happen."

Ezell could have tossed David's tray on the ground but quickly considered the consequences. He decided to use his words instead. "My dad does not control my life. I'm gonna do what's best for me." He then placed his briefcase on the table, sorting through the neatly placed papers inside.

Franklin gave a look of disbelief. "Is he gonna let you get into music?" he asked.

Ezell shook his head. "He said real men don't make music for a living. I don't want to do it for a living, but it's a gift I have, so I may as well use it for something."

David and Franklin glanced at each other. "Mr. Blair won't try to sneak us no surprises today, will he?" the former asked.

Ezell had taken out the paper with the geography questions and answers on it. "He thinks he is," he replied with a smirk.

The cheerleader Ezell thought he had been flirting with earlier was now wearing the varsity letter jacket of one of the football players. Ezell watched her lay on the wide receiver from afar. This girl was clearly not the one for him. Ezell was not exactly as delusional as he would pretend to be, but there had been times when he felt a mutual infatuation with someone, only for them to choose another guy—a bigger guy.

He never made a big deal out of it for the simple reason that, aside from his size, Ezell could not fight, a fact he was unapologetically candid about. The truth was that he never had a reason to fight. While his father was away in the war, he was taught to be well mannered by his mother and grandmother. When Ezell Sr. returned from India, he was determined to establish his position as the dominant force in the household, meaning he was responsible for protecting everyone, including Ezell.

\*

Ezell was still trying to discover himself as a man without following his father's template. To become a man in this society, you needed a woman... or two or three. "Junior," his father's voice broke him from the trance he had entered just before walking into geography class. "I hope you'll focus more than that through this next hour or so."

Ezell sighed. It had been a long day, and there was just one more class to go—his father's class. "I'll try," he replied. "While we're out here, I want to ask you about... you know, what we talked about."

His father peered at him. *That talk? Oh, of course not, we had that talk a long time ago.* Then it dawned on him that Ezell was referring to the competition. "We'll discuss it later. Come on," he said.

Ezell seemed displeased. Everyone knows that most parents do not actually intend to discuss a topic after they say, "We'll talk about it later." It would not matter right then, but Ezell would press the conversation until he received an answer, as long as he could remain focused that is.

Ezell's seat was secluded from the others so that he would not cause a distraction to his classmates. Yes, the teacher's own son had to be separated from the other students at times. It was quite embarrassing for Ezell Sr. at first, but at least no one could complain of nepotism. Everyone was always exhausted by the end of the day. Ezell was the only student full of energy while his father prolonged a lesson on African deserts.

The instructor knew his students would fall asleep during the lecture and was ready to surprise them. Mr. Blair erased the board of facts on Namibia and Botswana. "All right, who's ready for a pop quiz?" he said, leaning onto his desk. He scanned the room with his eyes and was shocked to see the students slowly stopping themselves from dozing off. They quickly adjusted in their seats with pencil in hand. Some of them turned to give Ezell a smile of gratitude, which he tried to ignore.

Ezell Sr. glared at his son at the back of the class, but Ezell refused to make eye contact with the suspicious instructor he had to ride home with.

And live with. David saw the awkward, nonverbal communication and shook his head.

*Gotta love E.Z.*

*

Ezell placed the cartridge of the turntable over a shiny, spinning disc. He began dancing with an imaginary partner as Sheila watched from the bed. The purpose of the music was to drown out his enraged father's voice in the hallway. Corine and Adelia struggled to hold the swearing man back as he rampaged through the house. "I'm gonna strangle that boy!" he yelled.

Jean entered Ezell's room, exasperated. "Why are you always diggin' graves for yourself?" she asked rhetorically.

Sheila was confused about everything occurring at that moment. "What happened?" she inquired.

"Nothin' much," Ezell replied.

Jean gave her brother a look of disdain before turning to Sheila. "Junior gave the test answers to his whole class."

Ezell nodded, content. "Now Dad is in a fit of rage because none of his students are failing anymore."

Jean stopped the record, bringing Ezell to a halt, along with the music. "Junior, that's not the point," she said.

"Dad was clearly testing you when he left that paper out, and you disappointed him."

Ezell was ready to plead his case but paused when he saw his mother at the threshold. "Mom," he said ashamedly. She did not respond. Her eyes expressed enough disappointment in her son's actions. Jean and Sheila knew what this meant—it was time for a talk. They left the room quietly as Corine sat down on the bed.

Ezell would not have looked his mother in the eye if not doing so wasn't deemed disrespectful. His mother's way of discipline was mild compared to his father's methods but proved to be far more effective. Who could bear the shame of a mother's disappointment? "Junior, what made you think what you did was okay?" she asked. "Do you know that cheating could get you kicked out of college? And it's no way to get through life either."

Ezell was now ready to explain his actions, whether they made sense to anyone other than himself. "I just wanted everyone to pass the class," he said. "I don't see why that's such a bad thing."

Corine took a small breath. "Because success feels better when it's earned. What exactly are you learning in life if everything is always given to you?" she replied. "I understand you love to help others, but—"

The teenager had become impatient and interrupted his mother. "Then why are you upset with me? It was a simple mistake," he said in a more irritable tone of voice.

"Because some mistakes have consequences, Junior," Corine snapped. "Your actions can't be justified if you have to break the rules to get what you want, so when your father cools down, I want you to apologize for what you did." She was typically a soft-spoken woman, but when it was time to make her point, she did so effortlessly. Ezell knew he had likely done a disservice to his own character in trying to be a hero for his peers. He watched his mother leave the room as quietly as she came, taking whatever clothes she could find laying around the room on her way out.

Ezell put another record on before opening the drawer to find a brochure on A&T that Franklin had given him. He realized life was coming to him fast, and he would soon have to decide on where he would attend school. *Lincoln College it is. Far away from this place. Boom, decision made.* He closed the door to his room for solitude, then laid down on the bed. The sound of an orchestra encompassed the room as Ezell closed his eyes and romanticized the day he always dreamed of. The day he proved everyone who ever doubted him wrong. The day he achieved everything he'd worked hard for—the job, the wife, the family.

The day he became a man.

# Chapter Three:
# Visionaries

Ezell buttoned his black polo shirt. He placed a hat on his head and looked in the mirror. He put on the nicest jacket he owned, ironed every crease from his pants, and cleaned his shoes thoroughly. Today was an important day. Within recent years, after the bus boycott in Montgomery, Alabama, a campaign for equal rights had emerged from the African American community.

There was a man from Atlanta, Georgia who was chosen to lead the peaceful demonstrations in Alabama. Dr. Martin Luther King Jr. was a minister who believed in the method of nonviolence to challenge racial inequality in the South. This tactic had been introduced by Mahatma Gandhi to liberate India from British rule. Ezell had also been inspired by Gandhi, who proved that even the little guys could leave a big impact on the world. Dr. King was admired by many for his willingness to not only be a voice for the oppressed but to also stand on the frontlines and fight for the people, and he was now in Greensboro, North Carolina.

Ezell would not miss this opportunity. He had been informed of the leader's visit a few months prior. Dr. King would be speaking at Bennett College, a private school for women. It made sense that he would visit this institution, since the students at Bennett had participated in several protests, including an attempt to desegregate local movie theaters. Jean waited by the door for her father and brother. This was an event Ezell Sr. wanted his eldest two children to be present for, and they were all ecstatic about it.

Ezell's shenanigans from a few months before had been silently forgiven. His father did not hold grudges for long, and it was not his first time at the rodeo with his unpredictable son. Today was a special day. To get the chance to meet Dr. King in person, maybe shake his hand and express gratitude to him, was a once-in-a-lifetime opportunity.

And it was very unlikely to happen. Ezell was crowded into one of the classrooms at Bennett College along with his father, sister, and dozens of other guests who were part of the overflow crowd. David and his brother Frank Richmond were also present at the school, unfazed by the large turnout. Dr. King was speaking in the chapel, his message transmitted through the intercom of each overcrowded room. *Well, close enough I guess*, Ezell thought to himself. At least he could say he was on the same campus as Dr. King. Who else could say that? Probably many others, but it did not matter. What was important at that moment was the message.

Dr. King was being interviewed by two of Bennett's students. He had been asked how he felt about the nine children in Arkansas being tormented after admission into the school. The peaceful leader could only praise the young adults for being so brave and courageous, even under those circumstances. Ezell concurred. Those kids had to know what they were getting themselves into, but they did it anyway. They were all lucky to have walked out of that school alive. Not everyone got a second chance at life when they stepped out of line, and this very fact made for a smooth transition to the next question. The students inquired how Dr. King felt about the men who murdered Emmett Till.

This was a touchy subject, and it had to be a tough question to answer. *Do we all not hate those bastards?* Ezell and David sat up on the desks. They needed to hear the response clearly. Dr. King probably read everyone's minds. He knew this was a sensitive topic that could cause an uproar if his sentiment was even slightly misworded, but he knew what he believed in.

He explained how his entire character was built around patience and forgiveness, and that as a Christian man he felt one must love based on Christian concepts. Dr. King believed that if he were to allow himself to hate the men who murdered Emmett Till, then he would cause a disintegration in his own character. *Power.* That was the greatest word to describe this man's disposition. It was always worth noting that Dr. King was not just a talker. He never cared about being in the spotlight more than he was in the crossfire.

Ezell aspired to be like Dr. King, and, in a way, everyone did.

*

Ralph Johns owned one of the most popular stores in the city. It was a hot commodity for a few reasons, the main one being that a white man welcomed people of color into his establishment with open arms. Ralph was from Pennsylvania, where he'd rubbed elbows with people of all races. He saw the same vision for Greensboro. After the Brown v. Board case at the Supreme Court, businesses were supposed to integrate their services but were permitted to do so "with all deliberate speed," which really meant they could take as much time as they wanted to make the decision.

Many of Ralph's customers were students of A&T and Bennett College, African American children who admired Ralph and his love for people of all races and cultures. Ralph always encouraged the young adults to stage a protest in the city to end segregation, but to no avail. Most of them were too afraid and had parents who detested the idea of rebelling against authority, whether it was peaceful or not. The consequences could be diabolical. Ezell, David, and Frank were headed downtown to pay their older friend a visit.

There would be spectators surrounding the store every now and then. White men and women who could not comprehend why a successful white retailer would use his platform to help colored people. Ralph greeted three of his favorite customers with a smile. "E.Z., you hangin' out with the Richmond Brothers today?" he said.

Ezell leaned onto the bar of the counter. "Somethin' of that matter," he replied, "How's life?"

Ralph shrugged. "It's going well. Did you all go and hear Dr. King speak at Bennett College?" he asked. "I heard it was a huge turnout."

David nodded. "Yes, it was very empowering," he said.

"And hot as hell," Frank added.

Ralph looked at the three of them silently. As if a familiar idea had resurfaced in his mind. They knew what was coming next. "Well, since you all were so inspired, you should be ready to do something about the Jim Crow laws, right?"

David sighed. *Here we go with this again.*

Ezell laughed. "Why are you always goading us to be radicals?" he asked.

Ralph gestured toward a poster of Mahatma Gandhi on the wall. "I'm not telling you to be a radical. Nonviolence is an option as well."

Frank Richmond could not have disagreed more. "It's hard to be nonviolent," he said. "Do you know the men who murdered Emmett Till admitted to the crime?"

Ezell was baffled at the information. "Then why aren't they in jail?" he asked.

"They had already been found innocent, and after you've been acquitted for a crime you can't be charged again for that same crime," Frank explained. "That'd be double jeopardy."

This horrific news shook Ezell to his core. He had been delivering newspapers the summer that Emmett Till's mother, Mamie Till, had her son's photos published in a magazine. No parent should have had to see their child that way, but the world needed to see it. Ezell remembered vomiting over the bathroom floor, not necessarily because of the image, but to know the kind of world he lived in. The price you pay simply for being black. Franklin McCain recalled being suicidal at that time. He could not fathom that what happened in Mississippi might be all life had to offer him.

"I remember when they showed his picture in the magazine," Ezell said, solemnly, "he barely looked.... human."

The atmosphere had become heavy. Ralph was consistent in bringing a beacon of light to the racial tensions in the South. "That kid was around you guys' age," he said. "Don't you think you owe it to yourselves to fight for him? For everybody."

Ezell nodded. "You know I'm not much of a fighter," he laughed. Ezell did not do well in dark moments; he always felt the need to lighten the mood with jokes. "I've gotta focus on other things right now. You know I'm going to be famous soon, right?"

Ralph chuckled. "Are you still on about that singing competition?"

Ezell stood up to make an announcement. "In two weeks, I will be the winner of New Farmers of America!"

David could not help but glare at his obnoxious friend. "So, your dad paid your way in?" Ralph asked.

"No, he's delusional." David laughed.

"Yes, he did, so shut up, David!" Ezell yelled, smacking David in the back of the head. "Now I need to go practice with my band, because we're taking home that cash prize!" He gave a farewell wave to the shoppers, who could not have cared less what he was ranting about. "See ya later!"

Ralph could not stop himself from laughing. He thought Ezell was the funniest person ever. "See ya, E.Z., good luck."

Ezell exited the store. The sun would begin to set soon, and the streetlights would be on. His parents liked him home before supper, so if he wanted to meet up with his group, he would have to make it quick. Just as he was turning into an alley, a gruff voice called out to him. They did not call him by name though. "Hey, boy." Ezell had been called "boy" before by the wrong company, and he turned to see this very type of company trailing behind him.

A few of the white spectators who had likely watched him go into Ralph's store had followed him into the alley. They could only want one thing—trouble. Ezell had no time to conjure up an escape plan. There were three of them, and one had closed off the other end of the alley. He had nowhere to go. "Ole Ralph got y'all boys in there tap-dancing for tips?" one of them said. His presence and tone indicated that he was the leader of the group.

Ezell frowned in annoyance. "Ralph ain't like that," he replied, "he ain't like the rest of y'all." The cornered teen surprised himself with his response. He probably should have been more nervous in those moments, but if this would be the end for him, then there was no point in showing fear.

"You damn right he ain't like the rest of us," the leader said, stepping in closer to Ezell. "We only tolerate your kind because it's the law. You do know what the law is, don't you?" A small crowd had formed in the alley. Ezell now had witnesses, but more importantly for him, an audience of people who would judge the strength of his manhood by the way he handled this situation. *Do I know what the law is? Well, since you asked...*

"Yes," Ezell responded, "it keeps my people separated from assholes like you." That comment did it. The gang member behind Ezell kept him from making a run for it, so the leader could easily pin his target to a brick wall nearby. "What'd you say to me, boy?" he demanded.

Ezell could not break free from his opponent's grip. "Get off me!" he yelled, pulling the sides of the guy's arms.

The thug leaned forward and whispered directly into Ezell's ear. "I've got a nice rope and a tree in my backyard we can add your name to. I want you and all your *people* to understand that this is our city, our world, and you better stay on *your* side. I don't care what Ralph told you, whites and coloreds ain't meant to mix."

The demonic speech was interrupted by a familiar voice. "What's going on here?" Ezell was relieved to see Ralph parting the crowded area, David and Frank Richmond behind him. The gang leader let Ezell go almost expeditiously as David approached him.

"Well, if it isn't Mr. David Richmond, the high jump champ," he said in an obviously sarcastic tone. "You know this bum?"

David sized up his potential opponent. Though he was a meek guy, he would defend his friends by any means necessary. The gang members knew this would be a lengthy brawl, especially knowing that David was an athlete, and a prodigy at that. "I don't know what it is you're trying to do but leave E.Z. be. He don't want trouble." David's words may have been simple, but his glare said it all.

The disadvantaged teen knew he was not prepared to fight David Richmond, whose physical fitness was at a much higher level than his own. He took a step back and gestured at his friends. "Let's go, fellas." He said angrily. Then the trio filed out, making monkey noises as they turned the corner from the alley.

Ralph turned to Ezell who was lying on the ground struggling to breathe. "You all right, E.Z.?" he asked.

Ezell fixed his shirt collar. "I'm fine," he said. He was all right. Maybe a bit embarrassed, but he was all right. He watched as the crowd dispersed. That was not the ending he was hoping for, but at least he came out alive. Thanks to David.

Frank Richmond was livid. "How much longer are we gon put up with this?"

Ralph shrugged again. "That's a good question. I hate the way life is down here. It's nothing like Pennsylvania."

David's adrenaline was still running. "Well, maybe what you've been saying is right. Somebody's gotta do something."

Ezell was not half as interested in discussing politics after having a near-death experience. He was halfway out of the alley when Ralph called out to him. "E.Z., where are you going?"

Ezell waved back at them. "I told you, I have to rehearse. I'll see you all around." He walked down the sidewalk, exchanging smiles with the other citizens. He was always optimistic, no matter what he encountered in life. Ezell always portrayed an image to the world as the guy with an unbreakable spirit.

\*

He turned the corner into another alley just a block away, backing himself out of sight. No one needed to see him wipe his tears. What happened in the other alley should have been his moment. The moment he showed everyone that he was not weak, and yet, just a few years out from adulthood, he still could not defend himself. He still needed to be saved. Ezell gave himself a little time to mope, then it was back to being the optimistic guy.

Downtown Greensboro was the most diverse part of the city. You would see people of different races out in the open but hardly interacting with one another. Ezell saw a white man coming in his direction on the sidewalk and quickly stepped onto the road to let him pass by. That was a rule taught to black children in the South at a young age. He glanced across the street at the Woolworth's Store, a popular location in the city because not only was it a retail store, but there was also a diner inside.

There were hundreds of Woolworth's across the nation. Most people referred to these companies as *dime stores,* the reason being self-explanatory—most of the items costing a dime or less. According to the manager, Clarence "Curley" Harris, the location in Greensboro was the second best in the South. It was also one of the many businesses that had not desegregated, and Mr. Harris took pride in that as well.

Ezell made it to the railroad tracks. The tracks were placed oddly at a location that separated two different kinds of people from one another. African Americans had created a world of their own with their own doctors, lawyers, teachers, and such. It was not exactly fair that people of color would have less opportunities to succeed in life and typically received hand-me-downs from the white community, but that was just the reality everyone had learned to cope with decades ago.

Ezell knew it was too late to rehearse now that he had lost time back at the alley. If he was late for supper, he would never hear the end of it from his father. He paused on the tracks and saw that the sun was setting. This made him smile. At least he could find joy in knowing that a new day was coming.

# Chapter Four:
## The Rare Star in the Cosmos

Ezell was in a frenzy. He stood in the arts department along with his bandmates. They were all watching his tantrum with disdain. However, they were not surprised at the situation by any measure.

"What do you mean he didn't pay the money?!" Ezell exclaimed. "I thought this was taken care of last week!"

The lady at the desk scanned her finger down a piece of paper. "I'm sorry, Mr. Blair, but we did not receive a payment from your father at any time."

This was news to Ezell. Willie, Thurman, and John watched him panic with nonchalant expressions on their faces. This is what they had warned him about, and now the conflict was unfolding before them. Ezell pleaded to have the deadline extended, but it was too late. "You should enter the competition next year," the woman suggested.

Ezell shook his head. "I'm not gonna be here next year," he said. There was a cry of defeat in his voice. Who would have thought that, after nearly half a year of rehearsing, everything would crumble to pieces before him? His bandmates did.

"I told you your dad wasn't gonna keep his word," Thurman said. "You know he doesn't want you doing anything but following behind him."

The three of them had circled around Ezell. "There goes our chances at winning!" John said, ripping a flier about the competition. It was a bit dramatic, but Ezell understood their anger.

"Guys, I'm sorry, he was supposed to have paid the money weeks ago," he cried. "Had I known he wasn't gonna keep his word, I would have gotten a summer job and paid my own way!" This did not have the effect he thought it would. Ezell had hoped they would understand his situation. They did not have to trust his father, but they did so with Ezell's reassurance that the man would keep his word.

Willie had been silent this whole time. He turned to Ezell with the coldest stare he had likely ever given anyone. "It's our fault too," he said. "We knew your dad wouldn't keep his word, so we should have replaced you."

The words from the gang members a few weeks prior was light compared to what Ezell heard at that moment. *Replaced?* He had been exiled from a hobby he loved dearly. It was not like he could never pursue music as a soloist, but there was a sense of unity and brotherhood formed through the group. He wanted to explain himself, but there was nothing he could say to stop them from heading out the door.

Ezell walked into the hallway. *Is this really it?* Life had come at him fast. In those moments, he could feel a change in himself. He could not explain it, but it was as if something in his life had broken. It may have been his anger. There was no way his father could have done this to him. Ezell felt that perhaps all situations did not require a positive attitude, and this was one of those situations.

*

Corine was cleaning up the kitchen while her children did their homework at the table. Supper was over, and Ezell Sr. would be coming in a little later than usual. He was part of the NAACP, and they had a board meeting that night. Ezell was far more quiet than usual, and everyone in the house knew why. There was a sense of lifelessness in his eyes that his family hardly ever saw. He flipped through the pages of the geography textbook without an ounce of concentration.

The phone rang, slowly pulling Ezell back to reality. "I'll get it," he said. He finally had an excuse to leave the table. The call was for him anyway. "Frank?" This brightened his mood a bit. It had been over six months since Franklin moved back to D.C. The two of them did not talk often, but when they did, there was one question Ezell expected to be asked—*where will you go to school?*

His father had made it home, happily greeted by Sheila and Jean. Corine had placed a bucket under a leak coming from the ceiling. Ezell Sr. came to her side. "Why didn't you ask Junior to patch up that hole?"

The woman shrugged. "Does he know how to?"

Ezell Sr. was almost offended by the question. Of course he had shown Ezell how to patch up a hole in the ceiling. Any father would. "Where is he?" he asked in a stern tone.

Corine felt the tension rising even with just her husband in the room. When Ezell walked in a few moments later, she felt even more of a burden on her as father and son glared at each other. For the first time in a long time, Ezell was not smiling. He was not pretending to be okay. He was enraged.

"Come on, let's go get ready for bed," Jean said, escorting Sheila out of the room, swiftly. It was rare for a situation to escalate this far between the two men of the house, and they would not be present for it.

"Junior, what's been going on with you?" Ezell Sr. asked. "You've been catching the bus home all week. Is something wrong?"

Ezell grabbed the textbook from the table. *What a stupid question.* He would never say those exact words to his father, but his actions would. "Yes, something's wrong," he replied. "I think I'm gonna fail geography." The evil smirk afterward did it. Ezell knew where his father stood on education, and though he was passing all his classes, he had to test the waters. *What if I didn't care about failing your class?*

"What did you say?" his father demanded as Ezell headed down the hall. "I don't show favoritism. If you fail, then you fail."

Ezell shrugged. "Well, at least you can be honest about one thing."

Ezell Sr. brushed past Corine, who had been trying to de-escalate the conflict. "Everyone, just calm down!" she begged. "We can talk about this tomorrow."

Her husband had already stepped in front of Ezell. "So, you're an adult now?" he said. "You think you're gonna live in my house and complain about a damn singing competition when you're holding a B average in school?!"

Ezell stepped in closer. "So what? We practiced for months, and you took away our chances of winning—"

The man showed no remorse, interrupting his son. "I don't care!" he yelled. "I worked my ass off to keep a roof over your head. While I was off in the war you sat around here playing with dolls, and now you talkin' bout singing?!"

Ezell knew where his father was going, and he was ready to go there with him. "Well, at least I'm passionate about something!" he retorted. "Cause obviously when you have no purpose in life it turns you into a bitter, narcissistic man. I don't want to be an engineer, and I'm not going to A&T!"

Ezell Sr.'s anger had peaked. "I didn't ask you what you wanted. I'm trying to turn you into a man!" he shouted.

"No, you're trying to turn me into you!" Ezell had forgotten how heavy his father's hands were until one of them struck him across the face. He also never knew how much anger was locked inside of himself. Harbored emotions that would only surface in a heated moment like this one. They both were breathing heavily as if they had emerged from deep waters. The climax had come and gone.

"If you had any idea of the world you were born into, you'd know just how well off you are here," Ezell Sr. said. "There are people who could only imagine what it's like to have the family you have and the opportunities we lined up for you. I think it's time for you to go to bed and think about it."

Ezell went back to his room quietly. He had so much to say, but there was no point. His father never listened, and his mother just wanted to keep peace in the house. Ezell tossed his records on the floor. He had no peace if he was not allowed to be himself. Then came the big question everyone would ask themselves at some point during their life.

*Who am I?*

The sky seemed especially vast tonight, or maybe Ezell was imagining things, since apparently, he was delusional. He sat on the steps of the porch, looking up at the stars and contemplating life. He did not know where to go from here. He was a senior in high school still trying to discover his identity. At this point in time, he was just existing. The screen door opened, but he did not bother to turn around, since he knew who it was.

Ezell could sense his grandmother's presence anywhere. "You all right, Junior?" she asked. "I know a metamorphosis when I see one."

Her grandson took a deep breath. "Grandma, it seems like my life is just one big crisis," Ezell replied. "I feel like I'm stuck. What am I supposed to do?"

There was a flash from above them. Ezell looked up to see a streak of white light passing through the sky. "Remember when I told you that when you see a shooting star, something big is about to happen?" Adelia said.

"The only big thing I'll ever accomplish is graduation," Ezell said. "I don't think I can do anything else."

Adelia had sat down beside him. "Well, if that's what you believe about yourself, then so be it I guess."

Ezell sighed. "Everyone thinks I'm too weak to do anything, and they're probably right."

Adelia pointed at the sky. "You see how those stars crossed the horizon? No specific route, no direction, nobody forced them to move," she said. "They just found their way through the universe, adored by everyone who saw them pass by."

Ezell watched as a few more shooting stars ran across the sky. It was a breathtaking sight. "I don't know your destiny and nor does your father, mother, or anyone else," she continued, "and even if you don't know what your purpose is, just go wherever life takes you for now. If your intentions are pure, you'll find yourself where you're meant to be."

Ezell could always count on his grandmother, who was also his best friend, to give him advice to live by. Most times he could not make out what her analogies meant, but this one resonated with him on a spiritual level. He was still unsure of the decision he would need to make in terms of his future; would he go out of state for college or stay in Greensboro, close to his family? He had the rest of the school year to figure it out.

# Chapter Five:
# Redirection

Ezell sat quietly at the kitchen table. He had been there for several hours. Before him was the Lincoln University application, but he was reluctant to fill it out. Graduation was just a few months out, and he was still stuck at the dilemma. Just a few days prior, he read a newspaper article about Ritchie Valens, a musician who died in a plane crash just months into his solo career and, like Ezell, he was seventeen. The world was a scary, unpredictable place.

The young adult still felt deeply connected to a fellow African American brother who never received justice. Emmett Till had traveled far from home. He was likely a kid ready to see life outside of what he knew in Chicago. He was young, innocent, maybe even naive, but he was a child. And yet, in his final hours, there was no one who could protect him. There was no one to protect *any* of them. God rest his soul.

Ezell remembered he still had homework to finish. The application would have to wait. The final decision would have to wait. He would have to finish strong these last couple months of high school. Whatever he decided to do with his life depended on these final moments of adolescence.

*

Ezell stood in the hallway of Dudley High, home of the Panthers, taking everything in. He had lost good friends along the way, but apparently that was the way life was. People would come and go and no matter what, you just had to keep moving forward.

"E.Z.," this time it was a familiar voice.

Ezell turned around to see David approaching him. "What's up, David," he said.

"Nothin' much," David replied. He was in a seemingly pleasant mood today. Not to say he typically wasn't cheerful, but there was a light surrounding David at this moment. "Can you believe it? We're almost at the finish line."

Ezell smiled. "Almost." He noted, "Things are gonna be so different soon."

David nodded. "You know Frank and I got into A&T," he said, "we're still waiting on you." *There it is*. David was a patient guy and therefore gave Ezell all the time he needed to decide where he would further his education. However, it went a lot deeper than simply attending the same college with his friends. David understood the true meaning of friendship and would hold onto those bonds as long as he could, however he could.

"The world is an unpredictable place, wouldn't you say?" David continued. "There's so much we could do to make it better."

Ezell gave an expression of uncertainty. "Well, David, that's true, but we don't all have to be in the same place to do that," he said. "As long as we're all playing a part wherever we are in the world, then something's gotta change. I mean, what do we have to lose anyway, right?"

The reply made the two of them chuckle. Ezell could hardly take himself seriously even in his most honest moments. However, David respected his friend's point of view, reaching out his fist.

"Then let's do it," he said.

Ezell mimicked the gesture. "Let's do it," he replied, bumping knuckles with his friend. The two had joined forces, though they would likely be moving in opposite directions. As David walked away, Ezell turned to get a final glance of the school. Graduation was only a few weeks away. Then it was in just a few days, and finally, it came.

*

Ezell was finally a graduate of Dudley High School. He was surrounded by his loved ones after walking the stage to receive his diploma. Ralph Johns came by the Blair residence. He had become a family friend after working with Ezell Sr. on the NAACP board. Yes, a white man was fighting hard for equality for all people. That was a dangerous way to live at that time. The only thing racist white Americans hated more than colored people were white Americans who did not hate colored people. Ralph could not have cared less what people thought of him. He was a thespian, so to someone who had once devoted his life to theater, he understood that art could not be separated by color, at least not in the sense that society wanted it done.

"You've decided where you'll go to school yet?" he asked Ezell. The two of them sat in the living room amid a dwindling crowd of guests. "I hear a lot of children are heading over to A&T and Bennett."

*Well, of course, Ralph. It's right down the road.* Ezell knew Ralph wanted him to stay close to home. He even questioned if his father had bribed the man into talking him out of going up North. Even if that was the case, Ralph's motives for keeping Ezell in Greensboro were different than Ezell Sr.'s. Ezell's dad was being his normal controlling self, while Ralph only wanted to transform the city into something new but knew the idea involved young people. Ezell thought the idea was bizarre. *No one ever listens to children.*

The attempt to integrate Little Rock High School was a failure and resulted in an entire school year where all the other schools in the city completely closed down to prevent desegregation. In Ezell's mind, people were just wasting their time throwing children on the front lines. Though Dr. King was moved to see young people getting involved in the movement, he was not completely for the idea, as it was a risky task. He had children of his own, and no parent should have to bury their child.

Ezell still hadn't answered the question. "I'll go wherever life takes me," he laughed, "that's the kind of guy I am."

Ralph smiled. The answer was good enough. "Well, when you come home, make sure you come by the store and see about me, E.Z," he said. "And for the love of God, come back with a degree and not a kid."

The two of them laughed, and Ralph bade the family farewell. Ezell was beginning to feel a lot smaller as the world around him grew bigger. The people he saw everyday would not be close by anymore, and now he would finally have to decide if he was prepared to give this up to venture into the world alone or stay in his comfort zone for just a little while longer until it was the right time to leave.

In his bedroom, he found himself before the mirror again. It was as if he awaited his reflection to give him an answer. Next to him was the Jerry Mahoney puppet he had cherished all his life. At one point in time, he'd dreamed of being a ventriloquist. Now he was not sure what the future held, but the events of the past, his past, gave him sound advice. Or maybe it was just a fear of the unknown. Even still, from what he had experienced as a black child in America, from what he did know about the reality for people like him, adulthood would be horrific, and he would have no one to save him anymore. Yet, for some odd reason, and through the shadows of doubt, Ezell finally believed he would discover his purpose *somewhere* in the world.

And finally, the decision was made.

# Chapter Six:
## Dear A&T

The campus looked much smaller in the brochures. A&T was like a fortress full of fast-moving vehicles unloading families, suitcases, boxes, and whatever could fit for the journey, this *new* journey. Ezell had finally reached the biggest stage of his life—adulthood. He stood on the campus grounds, inhaling the scent of a freshly cut lawn and some other pleasant smell. It smelled like some kind of flower, Ezell was not sure what kind, but the fragrance could have only been worn by someone with fine taste. A few people had good taste at this school apparently, because as he opened his eyes, he realized he had been passed by a group of women—beautiful women.

"Junior!" Corine called out to her son, "call us as soon as you finish orientation."

Ezell gave his mother a warm hug. "Mom, don't worry, I'll be alright," he said.

Corine clenched the tissue in her hand. "Why did I think having you close to home would make such a big difference than you being in Illinois? I still feel like I'm sending you off to war," she cried, hugging him again and much tighter this time.

Jean rolled her eyes. "Junior ain't fightin' in anybody's war," she scoffed, "and please, for the love of God, don't drive your roommates crazy. *Share* the bathroom."

Ezell hugged his sister. "I'll think about it, Jean. I'll miss you."

Sheila came straight into a hug, squeezing Ezell as tightly as she could. "Junior, I'll leave the porch light on for you," she said quietly. "That means I'm expecting you to come home a lot."

Ezell laughed. "Is that right, Sheila? Hopefully I'll come home and you'll be doing your own hair."

Corine popped Ezell in the head. "Hush up!" she snarled as they laughed.

Ezell looked over to see his father bringing him a suitcase. "Last one," he said. "You know, the engineer program here is everything you could imagine it'd be. I must say, I hate that you chose to come here instead of Lincoln College."

The man's sarcasm was undefeated. "Dad, no you don't." Ezell muttered while taking the suitcase from him.

Ezell Sr. paused for a moment. All pride aside, this was a pivotal moment for them both. He knew it was time to be candid, if only once. "Junior, do you remember when you were a kid and the Klan put out word that they were active in Greensboro?"

Ezell nodded. "Yes, they said they were gonna lynch us and burn our bodies in our own yard," he replied.

"And what did *I* say?"

Ezell took a deep breath. "You said no one was gonna hurt your family."

His father never struggled to fight back tears. At times his family would wonder if he had emotions at all. This moment was no different. He did not shed a tear, but he was transparent. "Hopefully you can understand that although this school is my alma mater and I'm glad you decided to continue our family's legacy here, it was always more important for me to have you closer to home so I can reach you if you ever need me. I don't want to be intrusive, but it's only natural for a man to look after his family; for a parent to protect their children."

Ezell did not like these moments. It was time to go. "Sure, Dad, I get it."

Ezell Sr. smiled. "Alright, give me a hug. I gotta go do some yardwork."

The embrace did not feel very manly. Ezell did not want anyone on campus to see him being affectionate in that way, but he could not break free from the hug, and though he would never admit to it, he needed it. Corine was in shambles. "Don't forget to call me!"

Jean had had enough. "Mama, please!"

Ezell watched his family pull off the curb, leaving him there for good. After today, he was never obligated to be home at his parents' command, no one was coming back to get him, and he was free to make decisions without anyone's say-so. He could only hope he was prepared for the journey that lay ahead.

\*

The freshmen were divided into two extensive lines leading to a tent of their own. This was where the students would pick up their schedules. Ezell had stood in line for roughly fifteen minutes, which felt like eternity since the temperature was eighty degrees. He glanced around the campus to see any familiar faces, or unfamiliar, as long as they were beautiful women. It did not take long, in fact, most of the people in front of and behind him were Dudley High alumni. Ezell had just not been paying attention to his surroundings, otherwise he would have spotted the headlock coming.

"What's up, E.Z."

Ezell pulled down on the guy's arm to see who had ambushed him. "David?"

David released his friend from the chokehold. "So, you made the right decision I see," he said with a youthful smile.

"Did you get your room key?" Ezell asked.

David shook his head. "I'm not staying on campus, but when I do, I'll be crashing with someone else."

Ezell paused. "Who is *she?*"

David was offended. "Hey, watch it, you know I'm still with Janice."

Ezell shifted his focus elsewhere, awkwardly. He really did not know what David had been up to lately, but it would not matter now. What mattered is that they both had at least one friend on campus. After receiving his schedule, he and David went up to his dorm room to finish settling in. Ezell had become a neat freak over the years, so it took time for him to organize the room the way he wanted. David sat on the ground, stretching as if he was about to run an event at one of his track meets. "They put me in the dorms with all the athletes. Isn't that crazy?" Ezell said, glancing at the other side of the room that belonged to John Williams, his roommate. There were two baseball bats on the bed and a poster of Jackie Robinson above the dresser.

"So, what do you think about that Williams guy?" David asked. "He seems kind of off."

Ezell shrugged. "He seemed alright to me."

David shook his head, wondering why of all people he had asked *Ezell* about someone's sanity. "Well, I know you're wondering why you haven't heard from me in a while. There's something I need to tell you."

Ezell turned to face him. David was not an open book like him. He was a great friend but tended to keep his cards close to his chest. And now, he was ready to share something private. It would certainly snow that day.

Franklin appeared at the door. "And just what might that be, Hoppergrass?"

Ezell was ecstatic. "Frank!"

Franklin stepped into the room. "Glad you finally made it in, E.Z., but we can catch up later, we gotta get to orientation."

Ezell was curious. "Do you stay in this building?" he asked.

"Right down the hall," Franklin replied.

"This is who I'm staying with when I come to campus," David confirmed.

Ezell grabbed all the necessary paperwork for their meeting. "Cool, look at this. The three of us are together again."

Franklin rubbed the top of Ezell's head. "E.Z., don't embarrass us."

David and Franklin laughed as Ezell swatted Franklin in the face with the papers. It was the reunion they all needed. The days ahead would be challenging, but at least they had each other to lean on. Ezell had grown up with two sisters, and now he had brothers. They were all looking forward to finding their manhood on this new journey.

*

Dr. Martin Luther King Jr. was a traveling man, and many times did so with Fred Shuttlesworth and Ralph Abernathy at his side. They were his wingmen and close confidants. The three of their minds together would produce groundbreaking results. Both Ralph and Fred were part of the NAACP, and the former had helped organize the successful Montgomery bus boycott.

However, even the greatest idealists would hit a mental block every now and then. They sat in the hotel room, each separated into different sections and stretched out as if they were stranded in the desert. "So, no ideas?" Martin said.

"Martin, we ain't had any good ideas for a long time," Fred replied. "This movement has been stagnant for years."

Martin sighed, reaching into his pocket for a cigarette. "When we did the bus boycott, everyone came together. There's strength in numbers. How do we get people all over the South to get involved in this?" He headed to the balcony to light the cigarette. It had been a long day.

"Why just the South?" Fred asked, "What about the rest of the country?"

Ralph grunted. "Have you seen Alabama? If we can crack that state, especially Birmingham, we can change any city in the country."

Martin stood by the sliding door. "The question is *how*. How do we get people involved in the movement?"

Fred and Ralph glanced at each other. "Well, the children—" Ralph started.

Martin lifted his hand. "I don't know why I asked," he said. "I told you. It's not a safe idea."

Ralph groaned. "We understand your apprehension, Dr. King, but if we're gonna move this needle, we'll need people of all different ages to join in the fight."

Martin shook his head. "The battlefield is no place for children. This is up to us."

Fred agreed. "Martin is right. We don't even have all the support of our own people. The lady who attacked you with that blade was one of us. We can't afford to put kids in situations like that."

Ralph placed the pen on the table. "Well then, what do you suggest, Dr. King? Because we're out of ideas."

Martin stood silently as the cigarette ashes blew into the wind. "Patience is a virtue," he said. "We'll have an answer in due time."

*

It was the coldest shower Ezell had ever taken, even though the water was blazing hot. He stood there silently as the water streamed down upon him as if it was washing away everything he assumed adulthood would be. This was his life now. He could hear the crowd of football players entering the bathroom. They were excessively loud considering how late at night it was, but obnoxious athletes were always common. Ezell finally got himself cleaned and headed back to his room.

John was a lighter-skinned guy with curly hair from Virginia. He was not the friendliest person in the world; in fact, he was not friendly at all. He entered the room, threw his baseball gear into a corner, and headed out the door. He and Ezell had not said much of anything to each other since they met earlier that day. That was fine with Ezell, however, since he had other things to worry about now, such as waking up on his own, getting to class on time, washing his own clothes, making sure he ate balanced meals, studying, and going to sleep on time.

The list went on and on, and it brought the lad great anxiety. Even with his parents just miles away, they may as well have been on the other side of the world. Ezell stared at the ceiling for hours before he pulled himself together. This was still his chance to prove to everyone how strong and resilient he was. He had to excel at A&T, or else his Dad would be embarrassed by him. In Ezell's mind, everyone who knew him still believed he was weak.

And sadly, he believed it too.

# Chapter Seven:
# Culture

Ezell, Franklin, and David communed at the lunch table just like old times. David was abnormally quiet that day. Ezell and Franklin were too excited about how well the first day of classes went to ask him what was wrong. "So, we're all gonna take this ROTC thing seriously, right?" Ezell asked.

"E.Z., don't chicken out now," Franklin replied, "you know how you like to pass out when you don't wanna do something."

Ezell was not amused. "I'm not gonna back out, as long as it's the Air Force and not the Army. I'd fake my own death if I ever got drafted."

Franklin laughed. "Well, you better tighten up, cause if your grades start slippin', Mr. Blair gon' give you a one-way ticket to Vietnam."

"Now why would you even say that?!" Ezell whined. "I'm gonna be alright. I've got my entire schedule already made for the semester!"

"I got married."

Ezell and Franklin paused, staring at David, each other, then back at David.

"Huh?" Franklin said.

David sat up in the chair, finally prepared to break the news he had been withholding. "I got married to Janice." Ezell was caught off guard. This is why David had been so quiet. *This* was an insane time to break the news, just as crazy as it was to get married, he thought.

"Janice, the cheerleader from Dudley?" Franklin asked.

David nodded. "Yes, her. We eloped."

Ezell had to sit up in his chair. *"Eloped?"* At that time, getting married young was very common, but there was usually only one reason why a couple would elope instead of having a traditional wedding. "David," he said quietly, "is she..."

David nodded. "Yes, she's pregnant,"

Asking if he was the father would have been disrespectful to both David and Janice, but Ezell just could not believe what he was hearing. *David, a parent?* David Richmond could do anything, but parenthood was a different story. However, there was never a book on how to be the perfect parent, so all anyone could do was try their best. In those moments, Ezell could already see the effect the mere thought of raising a child at such a young age was having on his friend.

"Well, congratulations to you, Hoppergrass," Franklin said, "I know you'll be a great father."

Ezell agreed. "Yeah, I mean, look at the bright side. You're in college working toward a better future, y'know. You've already given your kid something to look up to."

David peered at Ezell. Clearly there was something else bothering him. "You do realize we're only attending A&T because we don't have anywhere else to go, right?"

Franklin shrugged. "David, it's safer for us to go to a school meant for people like us. Those white folks up in—"

David stood up from the table. "That's my point!" he yelled, "I'm tired of feeling like I live in a world they created for me. We should be able to go to any school we want and feel safe."

Franklin and Ezell could not have agreed more. It was rare for David to lose his temper, so when he did, they knew it was not directed toward them but out of frustration. "I get what you're saying," Franklin said. "I worked hard to get here, so I'm hoping it'll all pay off."

"What do you guys think is gonna happen next in the movement?" David asked. "You think Dr. King has something coming?"

Franklin shook his head. "Dr. King said it himself that the movement is dead."

Ezell was hopeful. "I'm sure he has a plan."

*

As the weeks went by, Ezell easily adapted to A&T's culture. The schoolwork was not too difficult, the issue was finding the motivation to complete it. When all the work was out of the way, then there was the fun part—the parties. A&T was always known as a place to have a good time, especially during homecoming weekend. Students would come together with their turntables in crowded rooms and dance until it felt like it was a hundred degrees.

Then there was the alcohol. Ezell threw all his morals out of the window during festivities like homecoming. He had already been having trouble with his roommate, who was always complaining about him leaving the room light on for too long. Ezell had explained that he only needed the light to study, but John was not an understanding person. He was, as the elderly would say, *not wrapped tightly in the head*. Ezell scratched the top of his head roughly before taking another drink. He refused to be stressed about anything on a night meant for celebration.

David often missed those events, as he would return home to check on his parents and wife. Franklin was not necessarily a partygoer, but he had found someone who made coming out on the weekend worth it. Bettye Davis was a student at Bennett College who had caught his eye. The two of them sat on a couch away from the other attendees. "How do you like North Carolina?" Bettye asked.

"You know I was born here, right?" Franklin replied. "This ain't my first time being here."

"But you were raised up North, and I know things are a lot different up there," Bettye replied.

"The South is ridiculous," Franklin said. "I can't believe people have put up with this *colored this* and *whites that* nonsense for as long as you have."

Bettye was a bit offended by the comment. "Just a second," she said. "The Bennett Belles have always fought for equality in Greensboro. In fact, we're planning on doing a protest sometime this year."

Franklin was impressed. "That's interesting," he said, "when exactly do you think you'll do it?"

Bettye sighed. "Our dean said we should wait till after Christmas, but honestly, I get tired of waiting. I just want to jump out there and make it happen."

Franklin agreed. He was so infatuated by Bettye's beauty and intelligence he probably would have agreed with anything she said. "Yeah, sometimes that's how you gotta do it," he said in a whimsical manner.

Ezell watched his friend slowly fall in love from across the room. It made him wonder if he would ever experience a moment like that one. What if the woman of his dreams was somewhere in the room waiting on him to ask for a dance? It was in that moment he realized he had never thought about the type of woman he wanted to marry. Ezell was a guy who could be blinded by a girl's beauty, completely ignoring all the red flags, and most times, he did not care.

*

He would certainly have a hangover the next day. He lay there on the bathroom floor, promising whichever deity listened that he would never drink again if he could return to his normal self. He had prayed this prayer many nights before, but he meant it that night, as he would likely mean it many nights afterward. It was at these low points where an individual questioned their own existence. Intoxication felt like a near-death experience sometimes. The door was halfway open, so Ezell watched all the students going to and from different dorms. *Why are we all here?*

Perhaps going to Illinois was too big of a move, but why was everyone content with being caged into these institutions designed to keep colored people in their place? It was an absurd concept, even without thinking deeply about it. Ezell was suddenly angry. He had given up his aspirations, his dignity, and a genuine taste of freedom to fit in with everyone else. It was safe to say the alcohol had given him too much to think about, but it had given him something to think about, nonetheless.

\*

Ezell entered his dorm room at the wrong time. His roommate was having the weekly heated argument with his girlfriend from back home. He eased over to his bed silently as the argument ended abruptly. This was the part Ezell hated the most, because now John's anger would be directed at him. "I take it since you've been drinkin' you won't have the light on all night," he said.

Ezell climbed into the bed, kicking his shoes onto the floor. "I hadn't planned to study," he replied, "but if I do, it won't be for long."

John glared at him. "I'm sorry for making that sound like a request," he said. "I'm letting you know that you won't be keeping me up with that damn light, Blair."

It was late, and Ezell did not feel like arguing. "Whatever," he murmured.

"I missed that, what did you say?" John demanded.

Ezell placed the pillow over his head. "Good night," he said, his voice muffled through the cotton. He thought universities were supposed to house people together who had similar interests and personalities. Apparently, they believed Ezell was a sociopath, but he digressed. The headache was already settling in, and thankfully he could sleep in the next day.

\*

Martin sat at the kitchen table before several papers. There was a newspaper article on the murder of Mahatma Gandhi atop of other newspapers. Coretta entered the kitchen in her nightgown. "Martin, it's late. Aren't y'all headed for Alabama in the morning?" she asked.

Martin sighed. "I can't sleep."

"Well, what's new?"

Martin began stacking the unorganized papers together. "Corey, God has placed something in my spirit," he said. "It's like I can see a wave sweeping over the nation."

Coretta frowned. "You don't think that means we'll lose the war, do you?" she asked, assuming he was referring to Vietnam.

Martin sat quietly for a moment. "I don't believe the *war* has even started yet."

Then Coretta understood. She sat down at the table, picking up the paper about Gandhi's death. "Remember in India how the African students weren't too sure about the concept of nonviolence? I think that's what the issue is for so many young people in America today."

"Fear is what's caused this movement to grow stagnant," Martin said. "We already know what could happen when someone is relentless in fighting for their beliefs." He scanned the article headline: *Gandhi Is Shot Dead.*

Coretta placed the newspaper on the table. "People feel powerless because being afraid is the mentality passed down from one generation to the next but look at what we did down in Montgomery. We were inspired by a man from India to use peace as a weapon, and it worked. It'll work again."

Martin placed a hand over his chest where he had been wounded by a deranged woman of color. "Last year, it became apparent to me that hate is something you can teach to anyone, no matter what color they are. That's why we have to push this movement for *all* people, no matter what it will cost us in the end."

\*

Ezell awakened suddenly in the middle of the night. This had been happening for quite some time now. He glanced at John, who was sound asleep, then at the window. Ezell's head began to itch again. His mother had suggested he see a doctor and make sure he was not allergic to anything, but he had not made time to do it yet. He looked out the window at the stars. There was nothing extraordinary going on up there, but he did begin to miss his grandmother Adelia. Standing so close to the window brought a feeling of darkness over Ezell, so he climbed back into the bed. He quietly hummed the tune of a Hindu mantra he had learned while studying Gandhi's teachings.

The mantra brought Ezell peace of mind, which is all he wanted.

# Chapter Eight:
# Cadets in Solitary

Ezell spent most of his time in class trying to make a better impression on his peers, particularly women, than his professors. He ran into one of his classmates while passing through the plaza and thought it would be the perfect time to approach her with all the confidence he could muster while wearing his ROTC uniform. *After all, women like a man in uniform.* Unfortunately, he was not her type. "E.Z., what are you, like ninety-nine pounds?" she said to him. "You wouldn't be able to handle me if you tried. Women like real men, not little boys."

*Well, that did not go well.*

As if the comment was not harsh enough, Ezell watched as the football players easily attracted this same girl and so many others subsequently after he was rejected. You would have thought he was used to moments like that after his high school days, but the truth was that it was still a triggering experience. Ezell put on a smile and glanced around campus, making sure no one saw insecurities surfacing in him. He had worked too hard to keep them hidden. He glanced over at the library and groaned at who he saw descending the steps. *Oh man, not him again.*

Joseph McNeil was a standout on A&T's campus. Even at first glance, one could note he was far different from everyone else. He walked everywhere with his head held high and was always on a mission to accomplish something, be it big or small. Ezell knew Joseph from the

ROTC program. Like Franklin, he was born in North Carolina but raised up North, in New York City to be exact. Joseph had graduated high school early and came to A&T on a scholarship. He would certainly make his family proud.

The women gushed as Joseph walked by them, much to the football players' dislike. There was something about when guys from the North came to the South that would drive women crazy. Ezell could never figure it out; in fact, he thought it was a dense way of thinking, but to each their own. He watched as Joseph corrected two cadets who were in violation of their uniforms and thought it would be a great idea to disappear before he was next.

Franklin came next to Ezell, also in his dress blues. "That McNeil can be a real pain, can't he?" he said.

Ezell shrugged. "I suppose he's just doing his job, since he's already been promoted to corporal."

Franklin glanced down at Ezell's head. The height difference made it easy for him to see the gray areas spreading from under the hat. "E.Z., have you been doing alright?" he asked.

Ezell glanced up at Franklin. "Yeah, I'm fine, Frank. You ask me that every day." His response sounded irritated.

"I'm just concerned," Franklin said. "You haven't been sleeping well for the last few weeks. If you need to talk about something, just let me know."

"Will do," Ezell replied, nonchalantly. "I've gotta get out of here to study, see ya later." He turned to exit the plaza.

The two cadets Joseph had corrected approached Franklin. "What's with that E.Z. guy?" one of them asked. "Why's he always passing out during drills?"

Franklin chuckled. "That's E.Z. for ya."

*

Ezell was back in the dorm room, staring at the words in the textbook, patiently waiting for the knowledge to leap from the pages and into his mind. He was so focused he did not hear John enter the room until the door slammed shut behind him. "Ole' dumb bitch," the baseball player murmured. Ezell took a deep breath, realizing it would be one of *those* nights again.

The rumor was that John had impregnated his girlfriend and was now in a frenzy. Ezell was not sure how true the information was, nor did he care, but he was concerned about passing his midterm the next day. "Hey, pipsqueak, it's lights out," John demanded.

Ezell turned to see his roommate gathering his towel and showering toiletries. *Just go away already.* He closed the textbook and took an even deeper breath this time. "Listen, John, I have a biology test tomorrow, so I'll likely be up all night—"

John was not interested. "And does it look like I give a damn about your *biology test*?" he retorted. "You better have it wrapped up when I get out of the shower."

He headed for the door as Ezell tried to hold his tongue. *Tried.* "I bet you wish you'd *wrapped it up*," he murmured, snidely.

John did a one eighty at the door, the silence between Ezell's comment and John slowly placing the towel on the table making the latter aware of the insult he'd made. John approached Ezell, who had backed himself into the wall. "What'd you say to me?" he demanded. Before Ezell could whimper a word, he had already been taken by the throat. John had a menacing look in his eyes, like he was looking into the depths of Ezell's soul.

"Maybe you forgot whose room this is but let me remind you of what's gonna happen if you disrespect me again." He tightened his grip around Ezell's throat.

"I can't breathe—" Ezell whimpered.

"Shut up!" John ordered. "You're a punk. *That's* why nobody respects you. Your family knows you're weak and whether they tell you or not, your friends think so too."

Ezell wished he could have toned out everything he heard but he used his strength to stop the tears instead. No man would ever see him break that way. "Now, again, the light better be out before I get back," John continued. "Unless, of course, you can fly."

He released Ezell, causing the smaller guy to wheeze for air on the floor. John laughed, taking his belongings to the showers. Ezell lay against the wall. He always seemed to end up where he started—alone and defenseless. Sometimes he would wonder how Gandhi and Dr. King could endure this type of behavior on a regular basis. Had they never thought about physically fighting back at least once? Because one thing was for sure—he was.

\*

Franklin held a sandbag as Ezell struck it repeatedly. David lay on Ezell's bed, laughing as his friend dedicated his life to every jab. "Alright, E.Z., I think you're good," Franklin said.

"No, c'mon, Frank, I haven't even broken a sweat yet," Ezell complained.

"E.Z., you damn near drenched," Franklin replied. "The whole room is hot because of you." He opened the window to let a breeze in.

"Shouldn't you be studying for your engineering test?" David asked.

"What's with you? You've been in a bad mood all day," Ezell replied. He sat down on the floor next to the bed.

David looked down atop of Ezell's head, noticing the expanding white patches. "E.Z., what's going on with your hair?" he asked.

Franklin turned from the window. "I've been wondering the same thing, but he don't like me asking him nothin'."

Ezell rubbed his hair. "My doctor says it's a rare condition that comes from stress," he said.

"What's got you *that* stressed?" David asked.

Ezell was about to think of an excuse when John walked into the room. It was silent for several moments, mainly because Franklin and David were waiting for Ezell to give an explanation. Finally, David decided to kill the awkwardness. "So, when are we gonna talk to Mr. Ralph about our protest?"

Franklin made an expression of discomfort. "Why do we need to talk to him? He's not one of us."

Ezell raised a hand. "Hey, easy on Ralph Johns. He may not be colored, but he's definitely on our side."

Franklin digressed. "Well, I think it's still a better idea to go downtown with the Bennett girls after Christmas."

David laughed. "That's a long time to wait. We can go right now if you want."

Ezell shook his head, dismissing the conversation as a whole. "It's too risky," he said. "Why would we put our lives on the line when it may not have an effect? Remember just a few years ago? There were students who did a sit-in in Durham, and what happened after that—nothing. They wasted their time."

Franklin was annoyed by Ezell's nagging. "But it's for a good cause, E.Z."

John agreed. "Absolutely," he said, while gathering his baseball equipment. The room went quiet for a moment. This shocked Ezell the most. Even his roommate, who was likely the spawn of Satan, agreed that segregation needed to be abolished. He probably should have organized his own protest to help release his anger. *No, never mind, that's against Dr. King's teachings.*

John looked from the window where his teammates waited for him. "I'll be down in just a second, guys!" he yelled. David came next to him, looking at the grass below.

"You reckon someone could land that jump?" John asked. David smirked.

John headed for the door. "I'll see you fellas later," he said, "and E.Z., I hope you get enough studying done *before* I get back."

He closed the door behind him as Franklin shook his head. "He's a weird guy."

David was going through Ezell's storage trunk on the floor. "E.Z., where's all the food at?"

Ezell climbed into the bed. "I'm gonna restock when I go home this weekend for my birthday."

"You'll be eighteen, finally a *legal* adult," Franklin said.

"Guys, I'm starving," David said, "I've gotta find something to eat."

Franklin laughed. "Go on down to Woolworth's and get you the five-star treatment," he joked, "they'll accept you with open arms, right E.Z.?"

Ezell chuckled. "They gon' send your ass back in a pine box."

The room, full of laughter, was followed by a deadly silence. The three friends remembered that this topic was a harsh reality for them. No film, documentary, news coverage, or paper could accurately portray the real-life events of racial injustice. They were trapped in a nightmare they could only imagine waking up from.

"Well, I'm gone," David said, headed in the opposite direction of the door.

"Gone where?" Franklin asked.

"I told y'all I'm hungry," David replied.

"Yeah, but the door is the other way, David," Ezell said. Then he watched as David climbed into the window frame. They were on the second floor. There was no way he would do it.

He did.

David landed on his feet in the grass. He stood, waved at Ezell and Franklin, and was on his way. Ezell stepped away from the window to conceal his admiration. David was not necessarily a daredevil; he was a risk taker. Ezell wanted to follow through with a plan at least once in his lifetime without being afraid of what could go wrong. Jumping out of a window was not on the list, but there were other ventures he wanted to explore but was terrified of failing at.

"That damn Hoppergrass is somethin' else," Franklin laughed. He was right. David was superman. He could take on any problem in the world with no fear.

# Chapter Nine:
# Until the End

The bathroom was like a fellowship hall for athletes after long days of practice. The baseball team would go at one time, the basketball players were next, and the football team would be last. People typically measured an institution's worth by their football team. It was sad but true. Thankfully, A&T had a great football team. The players conversed in a group about all the women they had been with over the semester. Typical athlete conversations involved women, their respective sports, training for their respective sports, and more women.

Charles was the football captain. He was in a different headspace at the time and did not want to be bothered with redundant subjects. In the middle of his teammate's sentence, he gave a random outburst. "Fellas, I think we need to do more to represent our school."

The other guys stared at him. "Charles, what the hell are you on about?" Tommy, the wide receiver replied. "You've been on this 'enlightened journey' nonsense for the last week."

Charles explained his statement. "I wanna be remembered for more than just football. Don't you know there's more to life than just the sport you play?"

He was hit with a collective "No" from everyone there.

"For most of us, football is our life. It was our way out," Tommy said. "Hell, I wouldn't be here if I weren't on a football scholarship."

Ezell entered the bathroom unseen and unheard by the other men, who notably looked like giants compared to him. He was carrying a pair of extra-large underwear that he hung on the rack by the door. Moments later, Tommy went to retrieve his towel from the rack and noticed Ezell's underwear. Everyone in the bathroom was at least half dressed, so he could not figure out who owned the drawers until moments later when Ezell emerged from the shower stall.

"These can't be yours," Tommy said.

"Well, they are," Ezell said, taking the underwear from the athlete.

The other football players laughed. "E.Z, now why would someone your size be wearing an extra-large pair of drawers?" one of them asked.

"Ask your woman, she knows why," Ezell replied. He exited the bathroom as if he had carried out the most divisive plan known to mankind. Insecurities would make an individual do the strangest things to seek revenge. Though the football team had not directly wronged Ezell, he could not fathom why women would shun him for athletes.

*Tuh.*

\*

Ezell slept restlessly that night, his mind pacing back and forth between all the world's problems. One thing college would do was show you all the trauma you'd bottled up throughout your childhood. His head was still itching and there he was, stressed, making the symptoms worse. The kick in the face did not help the situation either. "Ow, David!" he exclaimed.

"Sorry," David mumbled from the other end of the bed.

This was one of the weekends when David needed to stay on campus. Ezell did not know his visiting friend would take up so much space in a literal sense. Moments later, Ezell found himself plummeting to the floor. They called him Hoppergrass for a reason. He'd nearly knocked the wind out of Ezell with that kick. "Are you alright?" David asked.

Ezell had to catch his breath. "David, I finally got a break from my psychotic roommate, and now I can't even sleep in my own bed."

David patted the side of the bed Ezell had been laying on. "You *can* sleep in your bed. C'mon."

Ezell groaned. "Why don't you go sleep in John's bed? He's not here."

David declined. "I'm not sleeping in another man's bed."

"Oh, is that right?" Ezell retorted. "Why aren't you sleeping in Frank's room?"

David buried his face in the pillow. "He went home, and he forgot to leave me the key."

Ezell was not convinced. Franklin would have checked to make sure David was set for the weekend before leaving campus. He likely was under the impression that David would be somewhere else. "Did Franklin forget to give you the key, or did you just not ask?" Ezell inquired.

This irritated David. "Why are you complaining so much?" That's why your skin is breaking out now. Relax, will you?"

Ezell paused for a moment. Then he took a pillow from the bed, throwing it on the floor. "I guess there's just some things I won't understand until I become a parent."

David sat up in bed. "Huh?" he said.

Ezell took a blanket from the closet to make a pallet on the floor. David took the blankets from his hands. "What did you say?"

Ezell sighed. "I didn't say anything."

"What's been going on with you?" David asked. "For the last month you've been on edge for some reason."

Ezell pulled the blankets from David's arms. "Well, look who's talking," he said. "You haven't been to class in weeks, and you've missed most of your tests."

David glared at Ezell. "E.Z., you know I have a lot going on at the moment. My kid will be here soon, and I gotta find a way to support my family."

Ezell sat down on the floor. "Then maybe your priorities aren't in place."

David was fully awake now. "My child ain't even here yet and you're already calling me a bad parent."

Just hearing the accusation bewildered Ezell. He would never disrespect his friends in that manner, and David knew that. It was understandable, however, that David was under a lot of pressure and had likely thought this negative statement of himself. "David, that's not what I'm saying at all," Ezell said. "I can't imagine what it feels like to bring a child into this world, especially being as young as we are, but why won't you just ask for help? There's plenty of job opportunities on campus."

David sat on the floor next to Ezell. "E.Z., I don't know what I'm gonna do, but I know I have to be a man now. I need a real job, and I'll have to work harder than I ever have before, which means something else will have to give."

Ezell was startled. "Are you thinking about dropping out?"

David didn't respond. At least not fast enough for Ezell. Every second felt like a year in passing. "You can't give up," he said, "you're David Richmond. You can do anything."

David digressed. "I'm still only human, E.Z."

Ezell ignored the comment. It might have seemed selfish, but he looked up to David too much to even acknowledge the man's self-pity. There was also something haunting Ezell that he had trouble expressing. "David, listen, I know that we've been talking about making a change in the world, and while that sounds nice to say, I've come to the realization that some people don't change, so maybe some laws won't either."

David rubbed the top of Ezell's head. "E.Z., you worry more than me sometimes," he said with an honest smile. "I was never afraid of anything until I knew I was bringing a child into this dysfunctional world. But if this isn't the world I want my children to grow up in, then I'll change it to make it so."

Ezell took a deep breath. "You've got so much faith in people."

"No, I've got faith in myself, you, Frank, Dr. King, and anyone else willing to fight for our freedom," David replied. "Don't be scared. You won't be fighting by yourself, because you and I are in this together until the very end, E.Z."

*You won't be fighting by yourself.* These words brought an ample amount of peace to Ezell, even if it was only for that moment. "We gon shake on it?" Ezell said. "We gon go after whatever we want in life no matter what?"

David lifted out his fist. "Let's do it," he said.

Ezell returned the gesture, bumping fists with his friend.

"Let's do it."

Ezell watched David climb back into bed. "So, David, about my bed..."

"Goodnight, E.Z."

# Chapter Ten:
# Satyagraha

Ezell was always a fan of philosophy. He loved knowing other people's viewpoints on controversial subjects. This was one thing that made delivering newspapers so enjoyable during his early teen years. Because he had become invested in Gandhi's teachings, he put them into practice, applying them to his everyday life. Remaining calm in the face of an adversary was a skill he would need to master if he was considering doing a protest.

After a long week of classes, many of the students were doing their regular fun activities—parties, movies, drinking, and whatever else they could get into. Ezell, however, was going to bed. He was so exhausted he had not heard his roommate spazzing out on the phone until he'd already entered the room. "Are you sure it hasn't come yet and you just didn't notice?" John yelled.

Ezell knew exactly what that meant—the rumors were true. John was going to be a father. Again, Ezell did not care in the least, but he knew his roommate wanted to keep his own business hidden from the public. Ezell could now confirm that John would likely have to quit baseball and return to Virginia, and that alone was enough to unhinge the athlete. "What are you doing here?" he asked Ezell.

*Is that a serious question?* Ezell looked at the basket of clean laundry he had done earlier sitting next to his bed. Things were about to get out of hand, he could feel it. It was better just to stay with Franklin this weekend and give

*Mr. Psycho* time to calm down. "I'm just gonna grab my things and go," he said, walking toward the laundry basket.

John hung the phone up. "What did you hear?" he asked, angrily.

"I didn't hear anything," Ezell lied.

"I'm not joking around," John snarled. "Tell me what you heard, punk!"

Ezell could not move as fast as he wanted. He managed to gather a heap of clothes into his arms. "I'll be out of your way in a moment," he said. He hadn't noticed that John was locking the door. Then he turned and saw the window open.

"What are you doing?" Ezell asked, nervously.

"Getting you out of the way," John said.

Before Ezell could process what was happening, John had already subdued him. Ezell yelled and jerked uncontrollably and noticed they were moving toward the window. He struggled to break free from the hold, but he was able to make John stumble to the desk, knocking it over. Ezell wailed as hard as his lung capacity would allow him. "Somebody, help!"

Thankfully, on a college campus, no one would be in bed early on a weekend night. The students below Scott Hall could hear the commotion from where they were. "What's going on up there?" one of them asked.

People were standing outside of Ezell's dorm, banging on the door. "Are you alright?!" one of them said. "Someone, go and get an RA!"

Ezell was holding off for as long as he could, but John had the smaller guy halfway out the window. The students watching from the plaza screamed in horror. "Somebody, do something, he's gonna kill him!" they yelled.

"E.Z., is that you?" a familiar voice said from the other side of the door. Charles and Tommy had arrived at the scene. Ezell did not care who saved him at that point, he just wanted to live. The only issue was that the door was locked.

"We might have to break the door down!" Tommy shouted.

But they wouldn't have to take those measures now that an RA had arrived with a master key. "Hurry!" Charles yelled.

Ezell's life had flashed before his eyes several times during those moments. He may as well have been unconscious when the football players freed him from the jaws of death, pinning John against the floor as if he was being arrested. "Are you okay, man?" Tommy asked.

Ezell fell onto the floor. "Better than ever," he replied with a smile.

Then he passed out.

\*

The residential advisors did not have much to say about the incident. "We'll just switch you to another room," they said. Ezell was appalled at the decision. He did not understand why he had to give up his room, but his roommate was not being sent back to hell where he belonged. It was not worth making a big deal out of as long as he was separated from the lunatic, who wasn't even all that great at baseball.

There was an open spot in Room 2128. Apparently, there was a guy who had not had a roommate the entire semester. He wasn't excited that he would now have to share his personal space with a stranger, but he would get over it. Ezell made his way down the hall with all the belongings he could take at the time. He knocked on the door and took a breath to prepare himself for an awkward encounter. When the door opened, Joseph McNeil glared at Ezell as if he were trespassing on his property.

*Ah man, this guy?*

Ezell realized he had to say something, otherwise Joseph might close the door in his face. Joseph was a man of business, so Ezell cleared his throat to prepare a greeting speech. "Hello, I'm–"

"You're Ezell Blair," Joseph said. It came back to Ezell's mind that they'd crossed paths a few times in ROTC. Somehow, he was not surprised that Joseph was just as stoic outside of the classroom as he was inside.

"Yeah, you can call me E.Z.," Ezell said.

"*Blair*," Joseph said, "you may come in."

Ezell did not know if he should feel honored or offended. He pulled his belongings inside, examining the empty side of the room. He had been given a fresh start, hopefully this time with a sane roommate.

"So, listen up, Blair," Joseph demanded. "I've heard you like to start trouble, and I don't tolerate any foolishness, you hear that?"

Ezell shrugged. "Sir, yes, sir."

Joseph easily read the boy's sarcasm. "I'm serious," he said, "I'm here to give myself a chance at life and I expect you to do the same, so with that being said, we're gonna lay down a couple of ground rules."

*Rules? Nope. Send me back to the baseball maniac.*

Ezell could not believe that after two months of being set free from a controlling drill sergeant, he now found himself living with a younger version of his father. His parents had probably been praying for that to happen. For Ezell to end up in the care of someone who would keep him stable and focused. Joseph McNeil was the guy for the job, but he certainly had his work cut out for him if he wanted to keep Ezell under control. Without verbalizing it, the two freshmen agreed that it would be a long, challenging school year.

\*

Ezell went home the weekend of his birthday to attend church and spend time with his family. During that time, many predominantly African American churches also served as a rallying point for those who were part of the movement. Ezell thought long and hard about what the reverend preached about that Sunday. It was not uncommon for ministers to implement the struggles of black Americans into their sermons, but for some reason Ezell felt like the message was directed toward him.

After the birthday activities were over, he sat quietly at the kitchen table, pondering over all the people who had already been hurt or murdered for just speaking out against racial injustice. It did not take long to make a list of those names in his head. There were many. Adelia had sensed her grandson's low spirit earlier that day, since he was unusually quiet. She sat next to him at the table with a mirror in her hand. "Junior, how's school going?"

Ezell did not know how to answer the question. "It's a complicated matter, Grandma."

Adelia nodded. "Well, that's one way to avoid a subject I suppose."

Ezell laughed. Then there was an ominous silence. "Grandma, do you think sometimes people choose the wrong paths in life?" he asked, "I know you said that everyone has a purpose, but what if they live their whole lives fighting for something that isn't worth it in the end?"

Adelia sat up. "What's not *worth* it?"

Ezell didn't know how to respond without saying exactly what was on his mind. It was a good thing his grandmother could read him like a book. "Well, Junior, when Jesus gave his life, he did it out of love, even though he knew many people would still hate him."

Ezell sighed. "He risked his life for people who hated him. So, was it worth it in the end?"

Adelia handed Ezell the mirror. "Well, do you think *you* were worth it?"

She left him at the table to think. Ezell looked into the mirror, gently smiling at his reflection.

Ezell Sr. entered the kitchen to grab something out of the fridge that he did not need or want. It was just a reason for him to have a moment with his son. "Dad," Ezell said quietly.

Ezell Sr. came to the table. "You're an adult now, but you know I'll still knock your head off, right?"

Ezell laughed. "You'll have to get in line."

His father rubbed the top of his head. It was a contradicting action after he had just acknowledged his son as a grown-up. Ezell figured that perhaps, in a parent's eyes, children never fully grow up. He had not been a legal adult for a full day yet, and one thing he felt deeply was that he had a long way to go to become a man.

*

Franklin and David wrestled in the dorm room that was clearly not spacious enough for such behavior. Ezell steered clear of the horseplay, trying to focus on a book he had bought on Mahatma Gandhi. Regardless of the room's small size, Joseph managed to remain isolated from the trio. Though he was popular, Joseph was a loner. It had not struck Ezell until he was roomed with the scholar student that he belonged to no friend group. He was seen handling business on campus, and afterward he would disappear to the comfort of his room to prepare for the next day.

What most people did not know about Joseph was that despite his serious demeanor, he was what many would consider *odd*. Ezell could not count the times he walked in on his roommate quoting Shakespeare to an imaginary audience or playing chess by himself. Ezell often invited him out with Franklin and David, but he declined. Apparently "four's a crowd" was a more accurate phrase than it was not.

*Fine, whatever.*

Ezell was too excited to read about all the things Gandhi had accomplished in his life. He shared what he learned from the book with Franklin and David, who were not interested, at least not enough for Ezell. "This guy is a hero. You guys need to look more into what he did for his country if you plan on changing this one."

David yawned. "Different folks, different strokes, E.Z."

Franklin agreed, holding up his Bible. "I've been focusing more on the book we have here," he said. "I've been praying for all of us, and if we're gonna go downtown and do this sit-in then we need to keep praying, because when there are two or three people gathered in God's name, he'll be in the center."

Franklin meant no harm by the statement. It was only awkward because there were *four* of them in the room. Luckily, Joseph did not seem to be paying them any attention. "Well, it's about that time," David said. "C'mon, Frank, we gotta let E.Z. get back on his enlightenment journey."

"Shut up, David," Ezell replied.

Another awkward silence followed his friends' exit. Now Ezell was alone with the unfriendly introvert. He wanted to make the moment less uncomfortable for himself, climbing into bed instead of sitting at the desk where Joseph was. Once he had gotten situated on the bed, he continued reading the book.

"Satyagraha," Joseph said.

Ezell glanced at him. "Huh?"

Joseph still would not look at Ezell. Instead, he kept his eyes on the mechanics book before him. "It means *holding onto truth,*" he said. "That's the Hindu practice Gandhi introduced to help free India from British imperialism."

Ezell was more thrilled in that moment than he could recall ever being before. He just would not show his excitement. All this time, he *did* have one thing in common with Joseph McNeil, and they were both thinking the same thing about each other—*maybe he'll make a decent roommate after all.*

*Satyagraha* represented an individual refusing to change their beliefs even in the presence of danger. Every day, Ezell felt more confident that he was ready to live by this mantra, and it was good to have an acquaintance who already did. It made him wonder just what role Joseph would play in his life other than making it a living hell with his "active duty" mindset. It was mutual, however, as Ezell was sure that he annoyed Joseph more than the rising lieutenant had ever experienced. They considered rooming together a test, as learning to be patient with others was the first step to embracing the concept of *holding onto truth.*

# Chapter Eleven:
# At the Breaking Point

The holiday season was finally here. Students packed up their belongings and headed back home for three weeks of no schoolwork and, most importantly, no stress. Joseph boarded a bus to New York. For the most part, he and Ezell got along famously, and he had even taken a liking to Franklin and David. The four guys started out attending school events together, and over time they would all end up in either Ezell and Joseph's dorm or Franklin's to discuss politics. Joseph liked the idea of doing a sit-in, but no matter how many conversations they had about it, everyone would eventually get caught up in their everyday routines and the idea would be shelved.

Ezell's and David's home was right around the corner. It was now just the two of them again, walking around Greensboro so David could buy gifts. His wife would be having a boy within those next few months, and David was fixated on being a provider for his family. Ezell just knew the boy would be a junior. Sharing a name with a parent was a lot of pressure, because there was typically this undying need to live up to it. Ezell Sr. never let his son forget not to tarnish the *Blair* name that he'd made formidable in Greensboro. Ezell had done nothing to live up to his father's local legacy as an educator, army veteran, and NAACP chairman, and though he was known as the high jump champ, David carried an emptiness about himself. There was more he wanted to accomplish in life as well.

*Typical young-adult issues.*

"E.Z., have you been doing alright?" David asked.

"I'm fine," Ezell replied.

David was quiet for a moment, as if he was too guilty to say what he wanted. "E.Z, we haven't talked about what happened with your old roommate," he said. "I'm sorry I wasn't there to help."

Ezell sighed. "It's alright, David. As you can see, I'm still alive." This was normal behavior for David Richmond, who felt it was his life's mission to come to everyone's aid. Once he had formed a bond with someone, he could not stomach the thought of not being there in their time of need. Ezell did not need to be pitied, or at least he did not want to be.

"E.Z., that could have gone another way," David said. "I know you were defenseless, so I should have been there—"

"David, it's fine," Ezell said, "I don't need you to fight my battles, alright?!"

David nodded, realizing he might have been a bit overbearing, and Ezell knew he had probably gotten more offended than he should have. But they were willing to look past each other's subtle differences, as real friends did.

"I'm sorry, it's just been a long semester," Ezell said.

"Go get you some rest, brother," David replied, "I'll see you later on this week."

Ezell and David did their signature fist bump before parting ways. Ezell looked across the street at the Woolworth's store. There were people visible through the glass door such as the Caucasian customers seated at the stools around the counter while the African Americans waited several feet away. The rule was that coloreds were allowed to order food from the counter but would have to leave once it was ready. Dining at the lunch counter was against the rules for minorities in Greensboro as it was for most other cities in the South. "With all deliberate speed."

*Yeah, right.*

\*

Ralph Johns had come to spend Christmas with the Blair family. He was always welcome in their home. Of course, it would not be a normal fellowship dinner with Ralph if politics weren't a topic of conversation. Corine would excuse herself to the kitchen to avoid the debates the men would get into at the table about what would be the next steps to integration. Ezell was less intrigued by this subject. Christmas was supposed to be about family, so there was no need to spend time discussing an issue that could tear loved ones apart. He could not deny, however, that when he was alone, the urge to act against segregation weighed on him like an anchor, pulling him down into the depths of his deepest desires—change being one of them.

Ezell felt himself transforming into someone different and wanted the world to experience the same transformation, but if things did not go well, he would have risked everything for nothing. And who was he to speak out against laws that had been in place for centuries? No one. Yet, he thought of the story of Esther. She came from nothing, was later favored by a king, and managed to save her people from annihilation. For years, Ezell thought he was cursed to live during these times. In a world where the color of your skin would not allow you to be treated as a citizen in society, let alone a human.

But then he thought that maybe, just maybe, he had been born for a time like this.

\*

Joseph McNeil typically forgot the rules of the South once he crossed into Northern territory, or maybe he never took Southern laws seriously since he was so used to his life in New York. Either way, he was in for a rude awakening on his way back to North Carolina. While at the train station in Virginia, Joseph waited in line to buy something to eat, since he still had hours left to go on his journey back to campus. He might have been too hungry to notice customers, both white and black, staring at him in confusion. Joseph was waiting in the "whites only" line.

He approached the stand, prepared to order. The salesman hardly acknowledged Joseph's presence. He was completely discombobulated. "Alright, I'll take a hamburger, ketchup, mustard, and maybe just a few onions. I don't wanna get congested on the way home, y'know," Joseph's words went in one of the man's ears and out the other. The African American customers watching wanted to intervene. Joseph was clearly green, meaning he had little prior knowledge of what situations like this could escalate to. They thought the young man had a death wish.

"Boy, have you lost your mind, or can you not read?" the white salesman said.

Joseph was confused. "What do you mean?" he asked. He still hadn't noticed the crowd of people zoned in on the two of them.

"We don't serve coloreds here," the man replied. Then he pointed to a line of about twenty people on the other side of the station. "That's where you get your food from. With the rest of *them*."

Joseph was baffled, staring at the "coloreds" sign above the crowded booth. There was no way he could wait in that line without missing the bus. "Sir, my bus is gonna be here soon, if I don't–"

"That ain't my problem, boy," the man snarled. "I know you just got off that bus from New York, but we do things a lil' differently down here. We don't serve your kind, so go on over yonder before I have security carry you out. You're holding up my line."

Joseph glanced around the station. Some people looked away, probably to make the moment less embarrassing for him. It was, in fact, the most humiliating experience for Joseph, and as if the food stand conflict was not bad enough, shortly after he was forced to give up his seat to a white passenger on the bus headed for North Carolina. He would not have wished these incidents on his worst enemies–to be dehumanized, devalued, and treated as an outcast. That was a feeling he would never forget.

Joseph was not only naturally driven, but he was also impulsive. Once he was angry, his mind locked on to whatever or *whoever* offended him, and he would have his revenge. Even if it had to be done in a nonviolent way, people needed to know that Joseph McNeil would not be disrespected without consequences. He stood silently at the crowded end of the bus, plotting in his mind for hours before they finally saw the sign welcoming them back to North Carolina.

*This ends here.*

\*

The night everyone returned from winter break was an eventful one, as Ezell, Franklin, and David struggled to calm Joseph. The racist encounters replayed in his head so much that Ezell did not have peace of mind for weeks, and every day he watched as Joseph devised a master plan to cause an uprising in Greensboro. It was amazing how much you could learn from someone when they were in a vulnerable state. Joseph was from a poor family, dirt poor. The other three men could not relate to sleeping on the bare ground in a basement at any point in their lives, but Joseph had been at his lowest point several times, so there was no way out but *up* this time around.

Ezell did not know much about astrology. He knew he was a Libra and that apparently Librans could fall in love with many people at once. *Very inaccurate.* There was a stereotype that Ariens were hot-tempered and would not let a situation go until their payback was executed exactly how they wanted it done. Joseph McNeil was very much an Aries then, as he was adamant that the South would not view him as a pushover. He was smart, however, and knew he could not strike in a harsh or aggressive manner, since that was against the concept of *peaceful resistance* Gandhi believed in.

"Are we doing this or not?" Joseph demanded. "How long do you all intend to wait?"

Franklin, David, and Ezell glanced at each other. "Well, it is after Christmas," Franklin said, "so I guess we can get together with the students at Bennett."

David disagreed. "Frank, that's gonna take too long to pull together."

"So, what do you suggest we do?" Franklin asked.

The question was followed by a lethal silence. Everyone knew the answer. If they wanted to do a sit-in it would likely only be the four of them, and this very thought shook Ezell up in a negative way. He and his friends were sentencing themselves to death, all because Joseph wanted a hamburger. At least that's what he wanted to pretend it was about, but the truth was that denying minority citizens basic human rights should have never been legal in the first place. That problem went back to the day people of color were stolen from their homelands; they were never meant to be treated as humans in America from the beginning.

Equality was long overdue in the South, and someone had to do something about it.

# Chapter Twelve:
# The Night That Changed Everything

Ezell sat at the desk with an open textbook on engineering. His hands gripped the side of his head as if he had been forcing himself to stay focused. The quiet room was the antithesis of his racing brain. He wasn't retaining an ounce of information from the textbook sitting in front of him. Unfortunately, schoolwork was the furthest thing from Ezell's mind now. He was more concerned about his life.

The room door flew open, and he did not budge. Somehow, he had been expecting his friends to barge in and cause a commotion. He knew time was finally up. "So, what are we going to do?" David asked.

"We'll go over it one more time," Joseph replied.

Franklin sat down with a pencil, notebook and bible. "The dime store, right?"

Joseph nodded. "E.Z. and David's friend says that's probably the best place to do a sit-in, since downtown is like the heart of Greensboro."

David shook his head. "Why is he only me and E.Z.'s friend?"

"Cause we don't know that man," Franklin said, "But if y'all say we can trust him, then whatever. So, are we ready?"

Joseph nodded. "I'm ready, I don't know about y'all," he said. "Y'all might be chicken."

Franklin laughed. "Not me, I ain't chicken," he replied. "Hoppergrass, are you chicken?"

David shook his head. "Nope, I ain't chicken."

Ezell wanted to vanish into thin air. As he figured they would soon direct their attention to him, Joseph did just that. "E.Z., why are you so quiet?"

Ezell ignored the question. *Am I not studying?*

David came next to Ezell at the desk. "E.Z., we're waiting on you."

Ezell jumped up from the chair in hopes of escaping the confrontation. "Guys, I gotta go use the restroom and I'll have an answer when I get back—"

Franklin stepped in front of him. "No, you're gonna make up your mind right now, E.Z., because we're doing this, with or without you."

*Without me sounds great.*

As fearful as he was, Ezell's heart could not take the look his friends gave him—an expression of despair. This action would not feel complete without everyone present there. How many rooms were there in the world with less than four corners? The number *four* represents stability and power, both of which were needed to withstand the troubles that would surely follow the protest.

Franklin and Joseph went to different parts of the room, now questioning their own stance in the matter. Ezell had made things complicated, as usual, but David stayed by his side. "E.Z., I'm sorry," he said softly, "I shouldn't try and force you to do something you don't want to."

Ezell turned to him. "So, you're not afraid?"

David nodded. "I am, but I'll be a father soon," he said, "so I'm more afraid of what my son will experience. I wanna spare him the life we had to live. I think that's all parents want—to protect their children."

Joseph had been reading the newspaper article on Emmett Till's murder. It was a horrendous crime, worsened by the fact that no one was punished for it. Mamie Till was not able to protect her child or get justice for him. That certainly did not sit well with the four of them. "You know, my parents told me I can do anything I put my mind to, but that I needed to stay in my place so things like this won't happen," Joseph said, holding up the newspaper. "But I believe some things really are worth dying for if it means someone else won't have to suffer the way we have."

Franklin stared at the face of the Bible, sweeping his hand over the letters. "What greater love than this, that a man lay down his own life for his friends?"

Joseph stood in the center of the room as if to deliver a verdict. Then he took a deep breath. "So, I guess the question now is, are we ready to die for this?" he said.

The room was quiet. That was the question they had all been avoiding asking themselves. Now, they had to confront it head-on. Now they *all* had to decide. After several moments of silence, David raised his hand, followed by Joseph and Franklin. Ezell was speechless, turning away from his friends.

"Well, I thought I was crazy, but y'all got me beat by a long shot," Ezell said. "I don't think I can tag along just yet." His humor would have seemed inappropriate to anyone else at that moment, but it was necessary to lighten the atmosphere for his comrades.

"E.Z., it's a peaceful protest," Franklin said. "We're not gonna incite violence."

Ezell disagreed. "You don't know what's gonna happen down there," he replied, "And if something goes wrong, then everybody in Greensboro is gonna hear about it."

"Good," Joseph said, "they need to. The whole world needs to, so are you in?"

Ezell glanced up at the ceiling. There was one more thing he needed to do before he could make a final decision. "I need to talk to my parents first," he said, "but right now I'm trying not to fail engineering, so would you please give this thing a rest for just a little while longer?"

The other three men dispersed, giving Ezell one final moment to decide. He gazed at the stars from the window, waiting for an answer. Ezell knew he needed to seek consultation from his family first. However, they could only offer him advice. The final decision would be up to him. If he truly wanted to be viewed as a man, he would have to get used to standing on his own instead of bending to the opinions of others.

*But as for now, to the Blair residence I go.*

\*

"Junior, what are you talking about?" Corine demanded. "You're gonna *shake up the nation?*"

The four men sat in Ezell's living room, along with his family. Ezell Sr. sat quietly in a chair as his son explained himself to his parents and sisters. "You should be proud of us, Mom," Ezell said, "we're standing up for what we believe in. That's a good thing, right?"

Corine was worrisome. "We don't need you to risk your life for us to be proud of you," she said. "We're already proud of you."

Ezell sighed. "Mom, I'm not doing this for you," he said, "this is for the *people.*"

Franklin concurred. "We're doing this for the oppressed. It's like what Moses did for the Israelites, freeing them from captivity. We want to see our people free too."

Corine glanced at Franklin, David, Joseph, and Ezell. She knew this was something they could not be talked out of. They'd made up their minds to go to war. "Have you considered the cost of what you're doing?" she asked.

"We've thought long and hard about it, and yes, ma'am, we're ready," Joseph responded.

"Junior, when have *you* ever put yourself on the front lines?" Jean asked, dumbfounded.

"College has made me realize that, though I value my life, it's not worth living if I'm not valued as a human. We have no choice but to fight now," Ezell replied.

Ezell Sr. had still not said a word. "Baby, are you gonna say anything?" Corine said. This was the moment of truth for Ezell. In all honesty, for all of them. Everyone knew Ezell was heavily influenced by his father, so it was likely his stance would change depending on what he heard next.

"Are you all really prepared for what you're about to do?" Ezell Sr. asked. "You keep saying you talked about it, but you do know there's a chance you'll be thrown in jail, or worse." The young men glanced at each other but didn't say anything. They held strongly to their point of view as Ezell Sr. continued. "One thing is for sure—if you all go down there to protest, your lives ain't ever gon' be the same, and that's *if* you come back."

He looked at David. "David, think about your son. He'll need his father."

Joseph intervened. "We've made peace with everything, Mr. Blair," he said, "we're ready for whatever comes with this."

Ezell Sr. nodded. "Even death?"

Again, not a word was said. David, Franklin, and Joseph were all staring at the floor as if they were locked away in solitary, reevaluating their entire lives. Then Ezell raised his hand slowly. He had made his final decision. He was going to Woolworth's the next day, and that was all there was to it. David smiled upon seeing his friend stand on his own for once. And though he would not express it verbally, Ezell Sr. was proud of Ezell as well.

*

Corine had gotten Ezell's outfit together. He would be dressed as if he were attending a board meeting with his father. "Mom, really?" Ezell whined. "This isn't a formal event."

"It doesn't matter, Junior, you're still representing this family down there," Corine replied. "I'm proud of you, son. You're my firstborn, your father's seed, and your sisters' best friend. We want you to be safe. You're a man now, but you'll always be my baby."

Ezell's eyes teared up. "I love you, Mom."

They gave each other a hug, unsure if they were saying farewell for good. "I love you too, Junior," Corine said.

Jean and Sheila waited for their brother at the door. "Don't let them folks scare you down there," Jean said. "Remember, you're a *Blair*."

"That's right," Ezell Sr. said, "represent us well."

Sheila hugged Ezell. "We're proud of you, Junior," she said before whispering in his ear, "just please, come back."

Ezell did not respond. He had never broken a promise to his sisters, and this would not be the first time. He did not know what would happen the next day; all he could do was hope he would see his family again. Then he realized he had not seen his grandmother the entire night. Just then Adelia walked into the hallway, coming just close enough where only Ezell could see her. She pointed her finger up.

Ezell was puzzled. Was something on the ceiling? He could not figure out what she was implying, but somehow, he knew that was all she had to say about what he was planning to do. Ezell smiled at his grandmother, then turned to join his friends outside. It was time to head back to campus.

*

The men had caught a ride with one of their acquaintances. Ezell sat between Franklin and David, uncomfortable. He did not understand why Joseph wanted to ride in the front so badly, knowing that Franklin needed a seat to himself. Thankfully it was not a long ride, and Ezell was in a daze anyway. What had his grandmother been trying to tell him?

The car circled in front of Scott Hall and the four of them jumped out, preparing to part ways for the night. "We're meeting in front of the library, right?" David asked.

"Yes, we are," Joseph confirmed. "C'mon, E.Z., before I lock you out."

Ezell was about to follow his friends into the building, but something above him caught his attention. He looked up at the dark sky and saw a shooting star. Then it came back to him what his grandmother had been telling him his whole life.

*Something big is about to happen.*

# Chapter Thirteen:
## Just Gettin' Started

It was Monday, February 1st, 1960. Ezell, David, and Joseph waited in front of the library. "Where's Frank?" Joseph asked.

"He had a meeting with the battalion commander," David replied, "but he should be here any minute now. I would like to confirm if we'll actually be ordering food or not?"

*Seriously, David?*

"Can we get to the diner first?" Joseph asked.

Ezell saw a tall figure coming in their direction. "There's Frank!" he said. His smile faded when he saw Franklin was still in his ROTC uniform, and just as he suspected, Joseph made a big deal of it.

"Why are you still in your dress blues?" Joseph demanded. "You know you can't wear your uniform when you're doing something political!"

Franklin brushed the inquiry off. "Well, hello to you too, JoJo," he said. "I didn't have time to change."

"Guys, let's worry about that later." Ezell said.

"What do you mean? So many people died for you to wear that uniform!" Joseph shouted.

Franklin held his fist out. "Well, today we might be joining them, so let's get this show on the road before the sun goes down."

David and Ezell put their fists where Franklin's was. Joseph followed along, though they all knew he and

Franklin would revisit the uniform subject later, even if it was in the afterlife. "This may be our last time seeing this campus," Franklin said, "so, whatever happens today, we know this is for a good cause, and in the end, God, just use us to do your will and may you get the glory from everything we do."

Then there was the prayer—the Lord's prayer. They quoted it as they left campus, crossing the railroad tracks that had kept the city divided for so long. They were on their way to the diner and likely on their way to their endings.

But they were on their way, nonetheless.

*

Entering Woolworth's was not awkward: any person of color was allowed into the store. It was a regular day of business. Many elderly Caucasian people were seated in the diner area. The African Americans were standing in the "colored section," waiting to be served. Ralph Johns' had told the four freshmen who had just entered to keep the receipts of whatever items they purchased to prove they were, in fact, customers. None of the shoppers in the store suspected anything. Students buying school supplies in Woolworth's was a normal thing.

Once they had bought their notebooks, pencils, and whatever other small items of their choice, they all moved to the other side of the facility where the diner was. It was not a far distance at all, but it felt like an eternity to all of them. Some of the white customers seated in the booth stared at the men, confused.

*What the hell are they doing?*

There were just enough stools next to each other for the four of them to sit together. They placed their items on the counter and sat down. The waitress was so bewildered she almost over poured a cup of coffee for one of the customers. Ezell took the biggest sigh of relief. He was still fretful of what would happen next, but at least they had made it this far. They all glanced at each other without saying a word, checking in to see how they were feeling.

The waitress approached them. "What do you boys think you're doing?" she demanded. "Get away from here. Don't you know where the coloreds are supposed to sit?"

Franklin pointed at the menu on the wall. "We'd like to order, please."

The waitress was startled. *You'd like to do what?*

"Listen, I've had a long day," the woman said. "So whatever kind of joke this is, I don't have time for it. Just get up and go on where you're supposed to be before I call the police."

"Call the police for what?" Joseph asked. "We've got proof that we shopped here."

The four of them gestured toward their items and receipts on the counter.

The waitress took a breath. "Now, I try to be nice to you people, but we have rules in this business that I have to follow." She pulled the diner menus from the counter and left to the kitchen area. Many white customers were gathering their belongings and exiting the store, using a slew of racial slurs as they left. Ezell thought their outrage was hilarious.

\*

Some time had passed before Curley Harris, the manager, stood in front of the building for some reason. He was as red as a tomato, knowing this sit-in would tarnish the good reputation of the store. Ezell felt bad for the guy, because he knew what it was like to work hard for something, only for someone to take it away. He was ready to leave the diner, but Franklin likely would have broken his legs had he tried to move from the seat.

A black cook came from the kitchen, pleading for them to leave. "Look here, don't give them another reason to say bad things about our people," she said. "Go on back to campus before things get out of hand."

"Things have been out of hand, that's why we're here," Joseph said. "So, when can we expect to be served?"

Curley entered the building. "The police are here," he announced to the few white customers who were still seated. Then he approached the counter. "I hate to have you all arrested, but you're disrupting my business. We're ranked as the second-best dime store in the South, and y'all are here trying to take that title away from me."

Franklin shrugged. "Well, you do know it's illegal to deny service to people of color."

Curley dismissed the statement. "I can deny service to whoever I'd like," he retorted. "The law says I'm not obligated to change the rules of *my* store just yet."

Joseph nodded. "Well, then I guess we'll be waiting until you decide to make that change," he replied.

That comment clearly offended Curley. *Who do these guys think they are?* Shortly after, a police officer entered the building. In his hand was a billy club. Ezell winced, convinced the police were there for one reason. He could have wet himself when the officer came behind them to talk to Curley. David placed his hand on Ezell's shoulder. "Calm down, E.Z., this is what we came for."

An elderly Caucasian woman came toward Joseph and Franklin, placing her hands on their backs. The two men were prepared to defend themselves from whatever asinine comment someone who was well adjusted to segregation had to make. This lady had clearly been around long before the idea of integration was conceived. However, they were met with a warm smile and were shocked by her following words. "I'm disappointed in you, young men," she said. "It should not have taken you this long to do what you're doing."

The lady patted their backs and was then on her way out. Joseph and Franklin stared at each other, baffled but mostly inspired. That memory would certainly live with them for the rest of their lives, even if that was not long. Curley had finished explaining the situation to the officer. All the spectating customers waited to see what would happen next.

Ezell, David, Franklin, and Joseph were waiting as well. The police walked back and forth behind their chairs, hitting the baton into his hand. The sound mimicked a metronome, as well as the ticking of the clock above them. They had been there for nearly an hour and had not been served. The officer was having a hard time trying to intimidate them as he paced back and forth. The students had not broken any law, but they were not following the rules of the diner. Yet still, arresting them would have been too much of a job on its own.

Curley grew impatient once he saw the officer being hesitant. He went behind the counter to grab a sign. *Closed.* "Sorry for the inconvenience, but Woolworth's will be closing early tonight," he announced, directing his attention to the four customers in front of him. "You fellas have a good night."

Ezell smirked, "But we still haven't been served yet."

Curley ignored the remark, going back into the kitchen. The gentlemen looked around to see people grabbing their belongings. There was a crowd of people watching from outside. The word had spread quickly. Some of the men outside had cameras, and Ezell knew exactly who they were—friends of Ralph Johns. Ralph knew a woman named Jo Spivey who was a reporter in Greensboro. That must have been his plan all along, to have her come downtown to cover the story, because from the look of it, it would definitely be one by the next day.

*Well, is that it?*

That was not exactly how they imagined the day would end, but it was time for them to head back to campus. They came out of the building, stared down by both black and white spectators who assumed the students had lost their minds. This made David and Joseph feel empowered. *That* was the reaction they wanted. Franklin and Ezell had been taken by the approaching cameraman.

*Click.*

Jo Spivey emerged from the crowd, pen and paper in hand. "Are you the students from A&T Ralph told me about?" she asked.

Joseph nodded. "Yes, we are."

Jo jotted the response down as quickly as possible. "Were you served?" she asked.

"No, we were not," David replied. He was still hungry.

Curley Harris watched from the storefront. He hoped this fiasco would blow over and that he would never have to see those *troublemakers* again.

"Will you all be back tomorrow?" Jo asked.

"Yes, we will," Joseph said, turning to look at Curley, "and we'll keep coming back until you decide to serve us."

\*

They were headed for the railroad tracks again, this time more jovial than before. "We did it, fellas!" Ezell exclaimed. "We survived!"

Joseph sat down on the tracks to catch his breath. "That's the most afraid I think I've ever been," he said. "How do you guys feel about it?"

David leapt up and down, as if he were prepared to run a four by four. "I feel great," he said. "I mean, I may be the high jump champ, but I think I just took the biggest leap I'll ever take. Nothin' can top this feeling."

Franklin stepped into the center of the tracks, staring at the sunset. "Yeah, but I don't think they took us seriously enough today," he said. "They think this was just a one-time thing, that we'll be too afraid to come back again."

Joseph stood up, coming next to Franklin. "Well, it's time to prove them wrong," he said. "Now we just need to get more people to come with us, but if we can't do that, we have to be willing to do this ourselves. The four of us." They stood, facing the sun as it descended behind the city. There was a feeling of fulfillment that came over each of them before continuing to campus. Ezell stayed back for a moment, reevaluating himself, as that was the bravest he had ever been in his life.

He thought it was possible then that the going down of the sun could represent the ending of one era, and when it rose again, the beginning of a new one.

# Chapter Fourteen:
# On the Battlefront

It seemed like a regular Tuesday morning. Ezell had almost overslept and missed his eight o'clock class. Joseph, of course, was up and out at the crack of dawn. Ezell had stayed up to continue studying for the engineering exam that he felt more confident about at that point. He was headed to the plaza, where he ran into Franklin sitting at a table going over notes. Ezell was so tired he had not noticed the students staring at him as he entered the plaza, many of them reading newspapers.

"You look like you didn't sleep well," Franklin said.

Ezell sat down, placing his briefcase on the table. "I lost two days of studying, Frank," he replied. "I can't get a *C* on my transcript." He laid his head down on the briefcase, hoping to get a nap in.

Franklin nudged his shoulder. "Aren't you and David supposed to be heading down to Woolworth's in a little bit?"

Ezell's voice was muffled through the thick leather. "Yes, but I'm tired, man."

"Well, that's too bad." David arrived out of nowhere, dressed and ready to go, but Franklin could see that neither of his friends had slept well the night before.

"So, we got anyone else coming down?" David asked.

Franklin sighed. "Well, JoJo and I met with the student council today, and they agreed to come down later on."

"Sounds good," David said, thumping Ezell in the head. "E.Z., you ready to go?"

Ezell would not lift his head. "Yes."

*No.*

Ezell pulled himself from the seat and took a deep breath. It had already been a long week, and the week had barely begun. "Good luck down there, fellas," Franklin said, "Joseph and I are going downtown after our evening class."

That was their plan—to spread the protest across Woolworth's business hours, having groups switch out like work shifts. David and Ezell went to the diner that morning with their books and homework to do at the counter where they were seated again. The morning customers were more mortified than the evening ones. Seeing people of color next to them so early in the day was a culture shock—a disrespectful one. They would simply have to get over their discomfort, because Ezell was far bolder than the day before. He was so focused on getting the schoolwork done he nearly forgot he was violating the store's rules.

David was half asleep, so Ezell had to nudge him every few minutes or so to keep him awake. His wife was around eight months pregnant at the time, and he had gotten a job down at the textile mill. Apparently, he had been working overtime for a while.

"David, are you alright?" Ezell asked. "You're not overworking yourself down at the mill, are you?"

David rubbed his eyes. "No, I don't believe so."

Ezell was confused at the response. That was the most sluggish he had ever seen his friend, which meant something in his life was weighing on him heavily. "David, it's okay to rest," Ezell said. "I can stay here by myself if you—"

David closed the textbook rather aggressively. "I'm fine, E.Z.," he said. "Don't worry about me."

Just by his response, Ezell could conclude that David was on a downward spiral emotionally. He was eighteen, married, and about to be a father, with a full-time job and heap of schoolwork. It made sense if he was suffering from fatigue.

However, David would not leave Ezell's side, especially since there was a brewing crowd of white citizens standing around the door. They looked as young as they were angry. Ezell closed his eyes and chanted quietly to himself. "*Satyagraha*, hate cannot drive out hate."

That was the only thing to relax his nerves. David was unbothered by the unwanted attention. He had ordered a cup of coffee to help keep him awake but was denied and told to go to the colored section. He and Ezell would sit at the counter for another hour or so until the next group of students came in.

*

Things would not go exactly as they had planned. When Franklin and Joseph returned from the diner that evening, they revealed that they were not supported by the student council. However, there were about twenty or so students who participated the second day, so there was hope. "So, we're going back again tomorrow, right?" Franklin said.

"And the day after that," Joseph replied. "This is what I expected. There's still a bunch of students afraid of being thrown in jail or killed, I get it. But the ones who are willing to join in are depending on us to lead them, so what are we gonna do?"

Franklin put his fist out. "We're gonna lead them, right?"

Joseph put his fist where Franklin's was. "Right, Blair?"

Ezell shrugged. "Cool with me," he said, putting his fist out.

Joseph glanced at David. "David, what about you?"

Franklin grinned. "We already know what he's gonna say."

"Let's do it!" they said in unison before bursting into laughter.

David smiled. Laughter was the best medicine, especially at a time like that.

\*

On the third day of the protest, there were people from all over the city gathered at the diner. Many of them were students, and many were citizens who wanted to know what the buzz was about. Either way, they were all there, taking up space. Many of the white customers had gotten there as soon as the store opened to sit down so that the protestors could not be seated, but that did not keep the students from coming.

Franklin was slightly flustered that day. He had wanted Bettye to come to the diner and was offended by her reluctance. However, he informed the woman that regardless of his feelings for her, nothing would stop him from protesting. It sounded great to say out loud, but Franklin was in love with Bettye at that point and hoped he had not ruined his chances with her.

Ezell could not keep his eyes off one student who stuck out like a sore thumb. He knew not every white person in the city was racist, but he was surprised to see the Caucasian girl entering the store with the students from Bennett College. She was, without a doubt, ravishing in appearance. It was such a shame, because there was a special word used for white Americans who treated people of color with respect. And that very specific word was being used quite heavily once the white students from the women's college joined the protest on the fourth day.

"Segregation now, segregation tomorrow, and segregation forever!" was being chanted more and more as the building became flooded with protestors. There were buses lined up in the streets and cameras posted at almost every angle inside and outside the building. The story was growing bigger every day and being broadcast on the news so that everyone could stay updated on what was going on at the local dime store. Curley had become frustrated, since he was unable to serve the customers who were not there to protest. He was losing dozens of customers and thousands of dollars every day, and that was part of Ezell, Franklin, Joseph, and David's plan.

There was a saying that money made the world go round, which was why the Montgomery bus boycott was successful. Many, if not most African Americans in the South got around through public transportation, so when citizens decided to walk instead of spending their money to be in a crowded, *colored* section of the bus, the city of Montgomery lost around three thousand dollars a day. They quickly changed their laws after that.

*

The sit-in had expanded from Woolworth's across the street to Kress's. That was the most African Americans anyone had likely seen in downtown Greensboro at one time. People continued to pour in as the story played nonstop in the news circuit. Bettye Davis made her way downtown, brightening Franklin's day. Ezell thought it was *that* moment when Franklin knew he had met the woman he wanted to spend the rest of his life with. Ezell still wanted to experience that feeling for himself, but now was likely not the time to focus on his love life, or the lack thereof.

Hundreds of people had participated in the student-led protests. The football team had even come to support the cause, sporting their blue-and-gold jackets while acting as security. At one point, the violence had gotten out of hand when some of the Caucasian civilians tried to attack a group of female students, prompting the football team to form a circle around the women to escort them from the building. The men said the Lord's prayer as they marched through the store, keeping the feeble protected within the wall of letterman jackets.

Ezell had been keeping his worried parents updated every day since the first sit-in. They were happy he was safe but shocked to know their son was leading the entire campaign with his friends. Joseph's parents were not as pleased to hear the news of the Greensboro uproar. They had not sent him to college to become a rebel, and now the four of them could potentially be jailed for civil disobedience. They knew there was no turning back at that point, so they continued to scout out people on campus to join their movement.

Around one o'clock that Friday afternoon, Curley Harris claimed to have received a call that someone had planted a bomb at an undisclosed location in the building. A police officer made the announcement through a bullhorn for everyone to disperse so that the store could be shut down. The building erupted in chaos with people rushing out of the doors, screaming, shoving, falling, and hoping to save their own lives. One of the African American cooks had gone out of the back door and spotted Curley Harris standing at a window on the floor above, watching people flee from the building. She wondered why he seemed so unfazed after receiving a "bomb" threat.

The fear subsided quickly once the students reached the sidewalk. They were now cheering in victory as they danced back to their respective campuses. Yes, the lunch counter was still segregated, but the unity it brought upon the people of Greensboro who had likely never imagined themselves participating in a protest was incredible. In just five days, the young adults had brought national attention to their little city.

The four students from the first day had encouraged many others not to be afraid to put themselves on the front lines of the movement, and that was worth celebrating.

# Chapter Fifteen:
# Troubled Waters

The members of the student council did make themselves useful in putting together a school dance to commemorate the memories of the biggest protest Greensboro ever had. There were students from every college in the city. As proud as everyone was, there had already been rumors of retaliation coming from the white community. It would be next to impossible to locate every single person who participated in the sit-ins, but there were four students in particular walking with targets on their backs.

Ezell was having the time of his life on the dance floor. Being out there brought back memories of when he and David were part of a boy's mentoring program as preteens. At the end of the program there was a party, and this is where Ezell and David would channel their inner Chuck Berry and Little Richard, fighting over the broomstick to see who the better impersonator of the legendary musicians was. David was not at the dance that night because Janice's due date was approaching, so he opted to stay home with her.

However, Ezell's first dance buddy was present. Jean took her brother by the hand as one of their favorite songs began to play. "Junior, dance with me!" she said. The two siblings began doing a dance they had likely made up in their living room, and it was fun to view from the side of the floor. Ezell's attention was caught by the same girl he'd seen with the Bennett students, and there she was again, this time alone. He could not figure out how she was comfortable being surrounded by people of color, since many times that could lead to a sticky situation. Ezell noted again that the young woman was beautiful, and if his words could not express that, then the look in his eyes would.

*Nope, snap out of it, E.Z.! This is a trap!*

Now the girl was looking directly at him, and when she smiled, Ezell felt his whole world caving in on him in the most romantic way possible. The gym was too crowded, so their distant encounter was interrupted by students who were not done dancing. Dinah Washington's record was getting everyone in the mood, and Ezell decided to do something he had never done before. "Hi, what's your name?" he asked.

The girl looked up at him, pretending like she hadn't seen him coming her way. "I'm Sharon," she replied. "You're Ezell, right?"

Ezell grinned. "Wait, you know me?" he asked.

Sharon shrugged. "Weren't you in the newspaper a few days ago?"

Ezell's mind went blank. *Duh, dumbass. Ezell, pull it together.*

"Yes, I was," he said. "Do you come to this side of town a lot?"

"I attend Bennett," Sharon replied. "My friends and I came down to the dime store to help you all the other day."

Ezell smirked. "I remember you. You kind of stand out, ya know."

The girl's face blossomed into red hues as she tried to hide her smile, but her eyes said it all.

"Would you like to dance?" Ezell asked.

Sharon held out her white glove as Ezell escorted her to the dance floor. Ezell always thought the moment in his head would never be anything but a fantasy, but it was playing out the way he had imagined. He was the prince, and she was his Cinderella. No one was paying them any attention, but it felt like the whole world was watching them dance in the center of the ballroom, which was also a basketball court.

Franklin and Bettye watched from the table. "That E.Z. done found him somebody, thank the Lord," Bettye said as Franklin laughed.

Charles and Tommy approached the table. "Frank, we just want to show our gratitude for what you and your friends have done," Charles said. "You really brought the city together."

Franklin surrendered his hands. "Hey, man, all glory to God," he said. "It was a group effort, so we're thankful the football team came and did what you did."

"I'd been wanting to do something to change Greensboro for so long but didn't know what to do," Charles said. "But you guys made it possible for everyone to be part of the change."

Tommy intervened. "With that being said, we know there's talks of retaliation from the white folks around here who ain't too happy about y'all trespassing on their laws like that. Apparently, they've got a hit out on the four of you."

Franklin still had his eyes on Ezell, but he was listening carefully. "I know what the Klan has been saying, but I know what I signed up for. We all do," he said. "I was raised in D.C., so it's gonna take more than a bunch of *talk* to send me back home."

That was the end of that conversation. Charles and Tommy respected Franklin's position on the subject and went for a handshake. "Let us know if you need anything," Charles said.

"Will do," Franklin replied, shaking Charles's hand. He turned to see that Ezell had disappeared. There were no questions to be asked of his whereabouts. Franklin knew exactly where his friend was.

*

Sharon's dorm was the standard college woman's room—clean, tidy, and bright. Ezell had not been to Bennett's campus since Dr. King spoke there a couple years earlier. He sat on Sharon's bed, examining all the family photos on the wall. Sharon had changed from her ball gown into nightclothes. Now she was sitting in front of the mirror, combing her curly, auburn hair. There was something about her that felt so familiar, but Ezell couldn't put his finger on it. He did not want to have to ask, but he needed to. "So, what made you choose Bennett?" he asked. "Well, moreover, what made you want to join the sit-ins?"

Sharon paused right as she was putting a pin in her hair. "You mean why did I choose to go to a predominantly colored school?" she asked.

Ezell chuckled nervously. "No."

*Yes.*

"What I meant was that you really put yourself in danger coming down there to help us," he said. "Do your parents know that you support... *us*?"

Sharon turned to face Ezell. "*Us*?" she repeated. Then it hit her. She got up from the chair and sat next to Ezell on the bed. "Ezell, I probably should've started with this when we were at the dance, but I'd like to say thank you for what you and your friends have done for *our* people."

Ezell's eyes widened when the woman's words processed in his mind. It was as if he had solved the biggest mystery in life as he examined Sharon's facial features more closely. "Wait, you're *colored*?"

Sharon shook her head. "African American, yes." She reached for a picture of a man just as fair skinned as she was. "My daddy could pass for white too, but neither of us would even dare try it."

She was exactly right about that. Her and her father could have sat down in any "white's only" section without being questioned. Ezell thought it was funny to think how Sharon was passing, whether she wanted to or not. It was remarkable that she did not take advantage of her looks and deny who she was, and it made Ezell admire her on a deeper level. "So, what's your dad like?" he asked.

Sharon laughed. "You'll likely meet him some day," she said. "He's always checking in to see how I'm doing. He's a bit overprotective, and controlling, and cranky, and he overreacts to situations before he knows all the details."

For a moment Ezell thought she was talking about his father. "Is that right?" he said.

"But he loves his family," Sharon added, "and he's always pushing me to do my very best. What about your parents?"

Ezell did not know how to respond. Sharon had summed up his homelife before he could pull his own thoughts together. "They're pretty cool people," he said.

Sharon smiled. "I figured so, if they raised you to be as brave as you are."

Ezell was lost in the moment. The connection he felt with Sharon was ethereal, and suddenly nothing happening around him—the controversy, the death threats—none of it mattered. Something sparked between him and Sharon on just their first night of meeting, and he hoped it would grow as the days went by. He thought that maybe everything he had gone through prior to that moment *was* worth it.

# Chapter Sixteen:
# Catalysts

Ezell hummed the melody to a love song as he finished getting ready for his first class. He had been in a daze for a week since the dance. Joseph watched him in the whimsical state from his bed. "Blair, it doesn't take much to woo you over, does it?" he said.

Ezell grabbed his textbooks from the desk. "Not when you're with someone like the girl I got."

Joseph stopped Ezell before he made it to the door. "Look, E.Z., we've already talked about this," he said. "It's not healthy to get attached to people so soon. You never know what could happen."

Ezell chuckled. "You wouldn't understand, JoJo," he replied. "Sharon and I are like two parts of the same whole. We've practically lived the same life. You can't deny that she's the girl for me. Can't you just be happy for someone else for once?"

Joseph grimaced. "What's that supposed to mean?"

Ezell sighed. "JoJo, you seem stressed," he said, "if you're worried about those death threats, don't let those crazy folks get to you. We've got the whole city standing with us, alright?"

Joseph did not respond, allowing Ezell to be on his way. All four of the men were walking on eggshells, whether they admitted it or not. It was a scary feeling to know people wanted them dead before their lives had really started. Ezell had a distraction, however, because he was in love, and this time he was sure the feelings were mutual.

There was a crowd of people in the common area of the second floor. Ezell saw two students badly bruised sitting on the sofa. One of them had been bandaged around his entire chest, while the other had a broken arm and a gash around his eye.

*What the hell?*

"There he is!" one of the injured guys said. "Ezell, you're the one they were looking for!"

Ezell took a few steps back. He was used to taking the blame for things, and most times he was to blame, but that day he was unaware of anything that could have happened. Charles was also present in the lobby. He approached Ezell quietly to explain what was going on. "Ezell, you know about the hit out on you, I'm sure. Well, a few members of the Klan thought they saw you and one of your friends walking last night, so they attacked them and threw them in a ditch."

*Holy sh—*

Everything made sense then. One of the men was around Ezell's size, so the Klansmen had mistaken him for their actual target. It was likely that even after they discovered they had the wrong guy, they continued with the attack just to send the message Ezell was receiving at that moment.

"Watch your back," Charles said. "A lot of people ain't too happy about all the attention we brought here."

The wounded men stood to their feet. "And nobody asked you and your ignorant friends to do a damn protest in the first place," one of them said. "Negroes were fine with the life we had before y'all went down there trying to be heroes. Now we all gotta pay the price for you bastards!"

Joseph had come from the room after hearing the commotion. "E.Z., are you alright?"

The students in the lobby were divided in their opinions on the matter. What the enraged victims were saying was true, but the sit-ins were done with good intentions, not to bring wrath upon the black community. "We just wanted to help," Ezell said. "Sorry, we didn't mean for all this to happen!"

His apology was met by a lot of swearing as both men charged at him and Joseph before the football players held them back. "Go on, get out of here!" Charles said. "We got this, don't worry."

Joseph pulled Ezell from the lobby and into the hallway. "Well, so much for the whole city being behind us," Ezell said. "Actually, just forget I ever said that."

Joseph laughed. "Don't you be scared now," he said, "the city wasn't behind us the first day we went downtown. We'll be fine."

Ezell and Joseph parted ways with the former heading to his physics class. Ezell found it hard to focus as he sat there daydreaming about who would be waiting for him outside once the class dismissed. It was the longest seventy-five minutes of his life, but finally he was able to see Sharon. She stood in the sunlight like the woman from the story of Tír na nÓg, prepared to take her prince to the land of eternal youth where they would live together forever.

*

The couple walked through campus holding hands and talked about their respective childhoods. One thing Ezell had noticed about Sharon his first time meeting her was her exquisite fashion sense. He was especially astounded to learn that the woman designed her own clothes. Sharon was a fashion major, a decision her father did not approve of, but she did it anyway. Women defying a man's orders was uncommon at that time, so Ezell was impressed.

"So, you wanted to be a ventriloquist?" Sharon asked. "You've gotta do a puppet show for me one day!"

Ezell laughed. "The key word is *wanted*," Ezell said, "my dad said that was an unrealistic job for a man."

Sharon disagreed. "I think the realest jobs are the ones you love doing," she said. "My dad didn't approve of me coming here for fashion, but it's what I love. You have to find your *own* path in this world, E.Z."

Ezell took a stressful sigh. "I'm tired of looking for the path I'm supposed to be on," he said, "I'm already overwhelmed as it is."

Sharon rubbed Ezell's hair. "I get it," she said, "those death threats are so unnecessary, but look at all the students in other cities protesting because of what you did. There's plenty of people on your side."

Ezell came to a halt. "What are you talking about?" he asked. "People in *other* cities?"

"Have you not been watching the news?" Sharon asked.

"No, what did I miss?" Ezell replied. "Are you saying there are other protests going on?"

Sharon was confused, wondering if her boyfriend had been living under a rock. "Yes, E.Z.," she said, "they're happening all over the South."

*

The volume was all the way up on the television at the Blair residence. There were at least a dozen sit-ins reported in several different cities. Corine, Sheila, and Jean watched the students seated at the lunch counters, smiling at the cameras, sure and proud of what they were doing. Tears streamed from Corine's eyes. "Junior, look at what you did!" she said. "Look at all those children."

Ezell walked slowly from the kitchen. He had been watching the tv the entire time without saying a word. Franklin, Joseph, and Ezell had been discussing the unfolding events for the past couple of days, and they were astounded to know that they had ignited a series of protests after theirs. It was a great feeling to look at the television and see all the brave young adults standing for their beliefs, ignoring the orders of angry racist citizens who were not in favor of integration. It was a great feeling for Ezell to think to himself, *Man, I did that?*

As he continued to watch the resilient students from Fisk University, he saw them ripped from their chairs, having boiled hot coffee and condiments thrown in their faces, physically beaten by angry white mobs who were not dressed in their white sheets, all captured on film. All while employees stood passively, enjoying every moment of the chaos. Ezell could not shake the feeling of anguish that came over him. He stared at the TV and thought to himself, *Man, I did that?*

*

The next few weeks would have several highs and lows for all four members in Ezell's friend group. Everyone on campus was enjoying the attention A&T received from the public eye. The school had received visits from Jackie Robinson and Langston Hughes, both of whom expressed their gratitude to the four young men for setting the civil rights movement back in motion. David was hardly ever around since his son had been born. Joseph and Franklin continued their regular lives as best as they could among the positive and negative publicity they were getting.

Ezell, however, could not control his nerves and had picked up a serious drinking habit. One day, while under the influence, he passed out on the campus lawn in the hot sun. Thankfully, Sharon was able to straighten him up before Langston Hughes approached them. The Harlem legend gave Ezell a signed copy of his book. He was not in the best state of mind while meeting an iconic social activist, but in those days Ezell's mental health was slipping. The amount of stress he was under worsened his psoriasis, and he began undergoing laser resurfacing to aid the skin condition.

Even with everything going on, Ezell managed to maintain exceptional grades which he became heavily concerned about, likely to distract himself from the chaos happening around him. There was only a month left of school, and though the college student sit-ins had ceased downtown, the high school students were protesting on a regular basis, along with anyone else who wanted to participate. The movement was on a roll now, with at least thirty thousand students in the South working to desegregate their respective local businesses.

One day, Ezell, Franklin, Joseph, and David had been pulled to the side by a professor who received word about an upcoming convention at Shaw University in Raleigh, North Carolina. It would be happening on Easter weekend, so Ezell wondered who could possibly think they were important enough to call a meeting on a holiday. There were few people he had enough respect for to miss Easter with his family, and Dr. King was one of them. Ezell was mortified to know that the leader of the movement had asked him and his friends to travel across the state and discuss whatever it was they would be meeting about.

It really didn't matter what it was about. That was the chance of a lifetime, and he would not miss it for anything.

# Chapter Seventeen:
# The Convention

"I just don't think it's a good idea," Ezell Sr. said. He had always been stubborn, but that day he was being completely ridiculous in his family's eyes. "You've done enough for the movement, now they want you to join in on their meetings? They're putting you in danger!"

Ezell sat at the table with his hands over his temples. They had been going at it for over an hour, and he had failed to convince his father he would be safe at the convention in Raleigh. "Dad, I'll be fine!" he said. "There'll be a bunch of other people my age going too."

Ezell Sr. dismissed the statement. "I'm not concerned about the other kids, I'm worried about my son, and I don't think political meetings are something you should be involved in at your age," he said. "I'm already tense about these damn death threats you been gettin', now you want to surround yourself with people going through the same thing. Someone's probably waiting for all of you to be in the same building so they can take you out at once!"

Corine swatted her husband's shoulder. "Honey, don't say that!" she said. "Junior is an adult; we can't keep babying him."

"Ain't nobody babying him, I'm playing my role as his father!" Ezell Sr. retorted.

"Well, I'm going," Ezell said, "I've already made up my mind."

The kitchen was quiet. No one had ever heard Ezell speak his mind in a way that made it clear his stance was unwavering. Even his father, though he didn't approve, was speechless. Adelia smiled, realizing her grandson was finally finding his voice before he had even noticed himself. Coming face to face with death every day made Ezell more assertive than he had ever been, and though the civil rights movement had made progress, there was still much work to be done. Ezell was excited about his chance to meet Dr. King and all the other young activists, but he was bothered by the fact that only two of his friends would be present with him.

David had continued to work overtime to take care of his family, so he was not able to attend the convention. People knew the men as the four students who reignited the sit-in protests, but only three of them were continuing with the work. David had decided to drop out of school to focus on his home life, which was falling apart. The fear of death lingered over his family, and he could hardly keep a job when white employers found out who he was. Then the racist townsmen would continually harass him at work, threatening to take his life and harm his family. Ezell understood why his friend had isolated himself from everyone and wanted to know what he could do to help.

*

"Just go on, E.Z.," David said. The two men sat in David's living room as the new parent fed a bottle to his son. "You get to meet Dr. King. This is your chance to really show the world who you are. Don't worry about me, I'm fine."

Ezell sat back on the sofa. "Alright, Hoppergrass, I'll leave it alone for now," he replied. "What's it feel like being a dad?"

David smiled. "It's the best feeling ever," he said, "the fact that my son was born in the midst of all this conflict proves that he'll carry on my legacy. Children really give you the chance to love harder than you ever have before."

Ezell reached over, tugging the baby's sock. "You wanna hold him?" David asked.

Ezell nearly panicked. "Who, me?"

David chuckled. "You are his uncle," he said. "C'mon."

Ezell rolled his sleeves up reluctantly. He could not remember the last time he held a baby, if he had ever done it at all. David placed the baby in his arms. "Make sure you support his neck," he said.

When the infant was finally adjusted in his care, Ezell felt as if he had unlocked a new level in the quest to find his manhood. He could feel the child breathing in and out, unaware of whose care he was in. For some reason, Ezell wanted the baby to sleep peacefully for as long as he pleased with no interruptions. He understood why David usually chose to stay home, because in those moments, Ezell himself would have done anything to keep the child safe.

"I told you, all a parent wants is to protect their children," David said. He placed his fingers over his son's chest, feeling his heartbeat.

Ezell's eyes teared up. "Wow," he said, "I can't wait until I experience this feeling with my children."

"You will one day," David said.

*

The day came for the meeting. Ezell, Franklin, and Joseph stood in the hallway dressed in the finest clothes they owned. This was a big day for the seventy or so people present at Shaw University. The gentlemen were waiting for instructions on when they could enter the auditorium, and as they waited, the other activists poured into the building. John Lewis and Diane Nash were two of the students who organized the student sit-ins in Nashville, Tennessee. They entered the building like they were on a top-secret mission compared to Ezell, who looked like a kid in the candy aisle.

"Man, I feel like I'm at a Hollywood film premiere," Ezell said.

"E.Z., who would wanna watch a movie about you?" Franklin replied while fixing Ezell's collar. "Besides, we can't let anyone show us up. Let's get serious."

Ezell laughed. He had forgotten how competitive Franklin could be. He always wanted to present himself as having his life together and expected the same from his friends. One of the administrators called for the students to enter the auditorium. It was time to see exactly what the meeting was about.

"Y'all ready?" Franklin asked.

"Let's do it," Joseph said.

Ezell was stuck in place for a moment. Something felt off, and it did not take long for him to realize how wrong it felt being at the event without all four members, even if David had told them to go on without him. He broke from the trance when he heard commotion behind him. People were crowded around the entrance doors to see whoever was in the car in the front of the building. "I think it's Dr. King!" someone exclaimed.

Ezell was too short to see over the people stacked against the glass doors and he wanted to get closer to them, but Joseph called out from the auditorium.

"E.Z., come on!" Joseph said. "I can't save your seat for too much longer!"

Ezell made his way to his friends. He knew he would have the chance to see Dr. King once the meeting started, and that was better than the last time, where he wasn't even allowed in the same room as the man. It was amazing how things had changed so much in so little time. Ezell Blair was about to meet with the bravest people in the nation, and he just knew it would be an event to remember forever.

*

And while the convention was, in fact, something to remember, it was extremely boring. Ezell was interested in the subjects being discussed, but he had a hard time sitting still throughout its long duration. Ella Baker was the main speaker at the event, or at least she was in Ezell's eyes, because she had the most to say. If Dr. King was like the father of the movement, then Ella was the mother, and one thing about men and women, they tend to disagree on things. The students felt placed in the middle of a disagreement between their parents because Dr. King believed the demonstrations required guidance by a higher authority, while Ms. Baker felt that the students could execute their own strategies without having any specific leader.

Ezell couldn't figure out how neither activist knew they disagreed on the subject before the convention was planned, but he digressed. Dr. King and Ella were, however, good friends, who still believed that the youth of the South would play a key role in solving the problem of inequality. That meeting in the spring of 1960 is when the Student Nonviolent Coordination Committee was formed.

\*

Ezell looked into the mirror of the bathroom. He had gone to refresh himself when the meeting came to an end after what felt like eternity. He could see the man he was becoming in his reflection. *Look at how far I've come.* The whole night needed to be commemorated, as it was the first time students had officially been pushed toward leadership positions in the civil rights movement. Ezell felt like he had made a little history, and after he exited the restroom, he would certainly have an unforgettable experience.

There were still many people chatting in the hallway, exchanging numbers to keep in touch before they parted ways. Ezell was about to meet up with Joseph and Franklin before he noticed someone coming his way. Dr. King was a busy man, so he was likely on his way to another meeting or to find one of his activist friends. Wherever he was going, he was in no rush to get there, because he stopped a few feet away from Ezell, fixing himself as if he was about to speak.

Ezell's legs began to shake, and his knees quivered and locked. Being in the same room as Dr. King already felt like a privilege, but now the man was standing directly in front of him. He had an intense energy that penetrated through the strongest of facades, and Ezell realized why so many people were intimidated by the leader.

Martin noticed the young man's apprehension and asked, "Are you alright?"

*Oh no.*

Ezell's brain was like a thunderstorm, raging out of control. He was not sure what to do or say. His mind raced between a million words per second before everything froze around him, and suddenly there was nothing. The last thing he remembered from that moment was total darkness and the sound of Joseph yelling in the hall— "For Christ's sake, E.Z., get up!"

# Chapter Eighteen:
# Worth It All

The last day of classes in college was much different than high school. People packed their bags and threw them into the trunks of their vehicles, and you weren't sure if you'd ever see them again. Ezell was strictly grieved to know this would be the case for Sharon. Apparently, she had made a deal with her father about maintaining straight As, and after receiving a C, she would have to transfer to another school she would not disclose to Ezell. He held the last suitcase as her father placed the other luggage in the car.

"So, this is it?" Ezell asked.

"I'm sorry," Sharon said, "I didn't keep up my end of the deal, so I have to go now, E.Z."

Ezell was baffled. "But I thought you wanted to be independent like you told me to be," he said. "You even told me to follow my passion regardless of what anyone says, even my dad. Now you're gonna give up fashion because you got a C?"

Sharon took the bag from Ezell. "E.Z., my dad is paying my tuition. I don't really have a choice but to do what he asks if I want to go to college at all."

"Then let me help you," Ezell pleaded, "I can get a job and—"

Sharon grabbed Ezell's hand tightly. "E.Z., stop it," she said. "It isn't your job to take care of me. Besides, you're busy doing all those good things for the movement, and

I'm so proud of you." She placed her hand on the side of Ezell's face. "And I know there's a girl out there who you'll make happy for a lifetime."

After she kissed him, Ezell felt dead inside. Sharon may as well have taken his soul with her in one of those bags. Just before she got in the passenger seat, she mouthed "I love you" to the distraught man, standing in solitude next to the car. There was no way she meant those words, otherwise she would have said them louder. That was the moment when Ezell wondered if she had ever loved him from the beginning, or if she had given him the time of day solely because his name held a great deal of importance in the city.

The car pulled off the campus, sending up a heap of smoke that didn't seem to affect Ezell at all. His emotions would not let him notice it. He rubbed the back of his head, right on the spot where he'd bumped it when he fainted upon meeting Dr. King. Thank God Joseph broke the fall just a little bit, otherwise he would have been unconscious. But even that would have been a better feeling than what he was experiencing right now. It was time to head back to campus so his parents could pick him up.

A group of women waved at Ezell as he left campus. He had grown immensely popular within the last few months. Before the sit-ins took off, attention from any girl would have sent Ezell through the roof, but he felt himself turning cold. There was no hope for anything anymore. At least that was how he felt now that he experienced a sharp pain in his chest, and though he figured the pain was heartbreak, he would not acknowledge it as such.

\*

The protests in Greensboro grew again once the college students went on summer break. People in the city did not think much about the consequences anymore. They would order their food to go, then sit down at the counter to eat. The county jail could not hold them all. Curley Harris wanted to find as many solutions as possible to accommodate his African American customers without integrating the lunch counter, but there was nothing up for negotiation. Either people of color would be allowed to eat inside the store, or the demonstrations would continue. The Woolworth's in Greensboro had already lost lump sums of money due to the protests, and if that continued, it would be due to segregation laws. Curley made a decision that would likely make him the most hated man among people of his race in Greensboro.

And on July 25th, 1960, the lunch counter in Greensboro, North Carolina was integrated.

\*

Ezell sat at the kitchen table with the newspaper in his hands. It was finally done. *Woolworth's Lunch Counter Desegregated After Five-Month Protest*. The African American community was ecstatic, but the feeling of victory was bittersweet for Ezell.

Adelia sat down next to her grandson. "Junior, you did it," she said, "I told you never to despise the day of small beginnings."

Ezell pushed the newspaper away from him. "It wasn't a flawless victory," he said, "I had no idea my life would have to change this much for us to get here."

Adelia rubbed his back. "Women come and go, Junior. You'll find the right one for you eventually."

Ezell sighed. "It's not just that," he said. "Even if people always remember me for being part of this movement, I still haven't learned whatever it is I'm supposed to learn in my life."

Adelia was concerned. "Well, what is it you'd like to learn, Junior?"

Ezell sat quietly, not knowing how to respond. Not knowing how to be honest about something he figured no one could teach him properly. He was not a man yet, no matter how much he was praised for being a *leader*. No amount of press or attention had filled Ezell's void. The journey to manhood was far from over.

"Junior," Ezell Sr. must not have been able to sleep either. He entered the kitchen and tugged his son's shirt collar, "You've done more in the last few months than a lot of people will do in their lifetime, and that's something to be proud of."

"*You're* someone to be proud of," Corine said. "Junior, there's only one way to go from here, and that's up." His mother entered the kitchen with her daughters behind her.

"My friends want to be just like you," Sheila said.

"Mine don't," Jean said. "It's alright though, they could never be as brave anyway."

Ezell laughed as his family surrounded him. "Thank you, guys, for believing in me," he said, "I love you."

Woolworth's was like a Thanksgiving supper for many people of color within the first few weeks that it was integrated. Caucasian customers were not thrilled to see the change take place and decided to stay away from the business, likely hoping it would return to its original policy soon. Ezell stood in front of the building to watch the joyful black citizens finally able to commune with one another, seated in the store.

Ezell understood that a seat was an individual's position of authority. He and his friends had taken their place as four trailblazers of their time, but as they said many times before, there was still work to be done. While acknowledging the people who came, and the people who left, at least Ezell could say that everything was worth it.

# Chapter Nineteen:
# The Dream

Ezell stopped the relentless alarm clock from driving him insane in his sleep. It was as if the device knew today was a day he could not stay in bed too long. Graduate school required a lot more discipline than his undergrad had. He had done well the last four years and was now attending Howard University in Washington D.C. Thousands of American citizens were headed to the capital that day to advocate for the economic rights of African Americans.

The Jim Crow laws of the South placed restrictions on African Americans, suppressing their access to equal public education, transportation, healthcare, and many other basic civil rights. Instead, people of color were treated as second-class citizens and were even intimidated through death threats to refrain from voting. The late spring of 1963 had seen a series of protests from not only adults, but children down to the age of four who wanted to be part of the change the black community wanted to see. This was especially true in Birmingham, Alabama, which caught national attention after footage of children being attacked by armed police and washed down the streets by water hoses of firefighters appeared on several news outlets, exposing the deadly, unsolved issue of racism in the South.

President John F. Kennedy was in office in the late summer of 1963. Just a few years before he was elected as president, Kennedy had verbally expressed his support for racial integration. After the sit-in movement took off, Dr. King had been arrested and jailed for trying to integrate a store lunch counter and was demanded to be released at Kennedy's command. He was a democrat who had grown up in Massachusetts, and many northerners were as oblivious to life in the South as Southerners were oblivious to life up North, so there was no wonder he was taken aghast by the footage of black Americans being tormented for participating in peaceful demonstrations. The graphic content made the president become more invested in solving the problem of discrimination in the Deep South.

Ezell got dressed and was on his way to the Washington Monument. He had only been living in Washington D.C. for a month, and he had not had time to see the obelisk in person, but that day he would. August 28th, 1963 would certainly be a date for the books. It was interesting that thousands of Americans of all races were joining to speak against racial inequality on the same day that Emmett Till had been murdered. It was a testament that the child's death was not in vain, and Ezell was proud he could be part of that historical moment. But as excited as he was to hear Dr. King speak, as well as climb the stairs of the monument, there were a few people he was even more honored to meet with again.

*

Franklin and Joseph waited inside the crowded national park, surrounded by what seemed to be every citizen on the planet. Franklin could hardly recognize his hometown among all the heavy traffic and pedestrians holding picket signs with phrases such as *We Demand Equal Rights Now* and *Give Us the Vote*. "Lord, I never thought I'd see the day people came out like this, but I'm glad I have."

"Never mind all that, where's E.Z.?" Joseph asked.

"JoJo, we've only been waiting a few minutes, give him some time," Franklin replied.

Joseph grunted. "We need to get moving before everyone else—"

Ezell tapped Joseph on the shoulder and went to the opposite shoulder to throw him off, but his friend knew better. That was a greeting only Ezell would give. "There you are, Blair, how was the ride?" Joseph asked.

"It was okay. So, are you guys gonna go up the monument with me?" he asked.

"E.Z., you're out of your mind," Franklin said. "Can't you just watch the event from here with us?"

Ezell was determined. "No, this is my first time here. I have to watch everything from the sky," he said. "Well, look who's chicken now."

Franklin laughed. "Whatever, E.Z., do what you want, but I'm not going up there."

"Has anyone talked to David?" Joseph asked.

Ezell's smile quickly faded. He was hoping no one would ask him that, but he knew he should have expected it. Franklin spoke softly. "The last I heard, he was having a hard time keeping a job in Greensboro," he said. "Those white boys won't rest until they can push him out of the city, or worse."

"You guys ready to go?" Ezell said, having nothing to add to the conversation. At least, not anything he felt like sharing. He could not remember the last time he heard from David, and as his life after undergrad became busier, he had not taken out time to find out what was going on with him. That subject would have to be dismissed for the time being so everyone could focus on the March on Washington for Jobs and Freedom.

*

Ezell remembered how out of shape he was long before he reached the top of the stairs. He would never admit to his friends that he reconsidered watching the program from the top of the monument. But he had made it, and he could see everything. The sea of people surrounding the Lincoln Memorial Reflecting Pool was a magnificent sight, especially given how hot it was that day. Men, women, the elderly, infants and children sitting atop the shoulders of their parents—all of them were there to support the rights of black Americans.

There were several microphones atop of the stands on the stage to be sure that everyone present could hear the music and speeches with no issues. Several people spoke, including James Farmer, John Lewis, and Roy Wilkins. The musical selections showed a lot of diversity, with performances by Bob Dylan, Eva Jessye, Joan Baez, and the one and only Mahalia Jackson. Ms. Jackson sang her staple cover of "How I Got Over" and moved the crowd with her thunderous voice that told a million stories of all the daily struggles black Americans endured. Listening to the words did make Ezell look back at what he had done at the lunch counter and wonder where he had found the strength to do something so courageous.

The program had been going on for at least two and a half hours when Ezell noticed that Dr. King had not spoken yet. He saw the cameramen packing up their equipment and wondered why they could not wait until the literal leader of the movement gave his address on the issue at hand. Shortly after, just as Dr. King was about to speak, Ezell noticed that there were a few more cameras covering the event, which made sense. You did not need a million cameras for one person. Dr. King began speaking, and the audience tuned in immediately. He flawlessly executed his views on the Jim Crow laws and how they were preventing the nation from progressing the way it should.

It was a great speech, at least the part of it they heard was. Mahalia yelled out from the audience, "Tell em' bout the dream, Martin!" before he could finish all of his points. It was known that Martin and Mahalia were good friends, but Ezell was shocked that anyone was bold enough to interrupt the leader as he addressed such a sensitive topic.

*And what is this 'dream' anyway?*

Martin looked back at his friend and smiled. Then he folded up the piece of paper he held, seemingly ready to switch directions. Ezell peered harder, as if a clearer vision would help him hear better. A few moments later, Dr. King began delivering a speech about his vision for the United States, a vision of unity between people of all races. Most politicians and activists relied on handwritten material, and it was said that Dr. King had not been the best at public speaking during his early years, so it was possible in recent events that someone had helped him prepare his speeches.

Not that day. It was evident to everyone present at the march that every word that came from Dr. King's mouth had also come from his heart. That was exactly why Mahalia encouraged him to derail from his common, direct and polished speaking and instead express exactly how he felt. His vision may not have been tangible right then and there, but when he was done with the speech, Ezell knew there would be thousands of people going home prepared to make it so.

*One day we'll make your dream come true, Dr. King.*

# Chapter Twenty:
## The Cost

The youth being involved in the movement proved to be an effective strategy. Children represented innocence, so when the nation's eyes were on the South's turbulent culture, President Kennedy started making plans to solve the issue, starting with constraining the integration of schools and businesses. The children had won. By 1963, it had become evident that young people had more power than they would have ever imagined, and for many southerners who would never accept integration, this would be a problem.

The 16th Street Baptist Church was often used as the meeting place for organizing the protests of the civil rights movement. It was where all the children who participated in the marches met and were instructed on how to behave during the demonstrations, and therefore it was also a target for the Ku Klux Klan. On Sunday morning of September 15th, 1963, several sticks of dynamite were planted under the stairs of the church directly next to the women's bathroom. When the bomb went off, there were five girls in the bathroom, four of whom were killed, and the survivor was terribly injured. The news of the hate crime shocked the nation and again proved just how immoral Southern tradition was.

*

Ezell had made his way to North Carolina. It had been over three months since he saw his family. The gathering was exactly what he needed. He sat at the table with his mother, grandmother, and sister, Sheila. Corine glanced at Ezell's black-and-gold wrist band. "Lord, I don't think your father will ever recover from you joining a different fraternity than him."

Ezell shrugged. "I never recovered from him not paying my way in to that music competition."

Adelia laughed. "How's school?" she asked. "You're getting closer and closer up North, aren't you?"

"I love it," Ezell replied. "I never knew being in a diverse area could really change how you think. No wonder Frank is so open-minded."

"Speaking of your friends, you know David had a little girl," Sheila said. "Her name's Lynn."

Ezell nodded. "Yeah, Mom told me."

"Have you checked on him, Junior?" Corine asked, "I mean, you're home, so surely you plan to go by and see him, right?"

Sheila agreed. "Cause I hear he's been really depressed since his last divorce. That was his second one," she said, "And the Klan has been threatening to kill him for so long hardly anyone will hire him cause most employers see him as a liability. It's like out of the four of y'all, he's been hated the most."

Ezell placed his fork down, slightly offended. "I don't know what I'm supposed to do about that," he said. "David and I have been friends since the seventh grade. If he wanted me around he would say it, but he's isolating himself from me and everyone else."

The table was quiet. Ezell's family could hear the pain in his voice. He had suffered from the aftermath of the sit-ins as well. Just the thought that young people were following in the example the four students from A&T had set and were now being murdered in cold blood was an extremely difficult burden to bear. And now, after everything he had persevered through, Ezell felt disconnected from his childhood friend, who was going through the darkest time of his life.

Adelia smiled at her grandson. "You're right," she said. "A man who wants friends must show himself friendly." She placed her hand on Ezell's back. "But there's a friend who sticks closer than a brother."

Ezell did not respond. The truth was that he feared rejection even from his friends, but he thought of how he felt before deciding to do the sit-ins three years prior. *Would it all be worth it in the end?* He'd decided to do the protest anyway and yes, it required a lot of convincing from his friends, but it was ultimately his decision to put his own life on the line for a greater cause. This time, he would have to truly stand on his own. Hopefully he could be the one to convince David to pull himself together, to remind him there was nothing the high jump champ could not do. Ezell had faith in David as his friend had had faith in him in the past, and he saw how the world was changing before their eyes. After evaluating everything, Ezell was ready to pay a visit to a lifelong confidant, his friend and brother, David Richmond.

\*

Janice was putting the children into the car when Ezell arrived at the house. David's son went by the nickname of Chip and bore an uncanny resemblance to his father. "Mama, it's Uncle E.Z.," Chip said as Ezell got out of the car.

"What's up, man?" Ezell exclaimed as the toddler ran to greet him. "What do you have here?"

Chip showed Ezell a tiny football. "I wanna play fuh-bawl!" he exclaimed.

Janice came, taking the boy by the hand. "Just like his dad," she said. She was carrying Lynn in her other arm, turning to introduce the baby to Ezell. "Lynn, say hi to your Uncle Ezell."

Ezell smiled. "My, oh my, David's got two now," he said, looking up at the door of the house.

Janice pulled the side of Chip's head to her leg and covered his other ear with her free hand. "I should warn you, he isn't in the best condition right now," she said. "Don't let much of what he may say get to you. He's just in a dark place, so he may not be exactly the David you remember."

Those words did not serve Ezell well, mostly because he was afraid Janice had confirmed exactly what he feared for so long. He never wanted to not recognize someone who played an intricate role in his life, which had kept him from reaching out to David for so long. He could stall no longer now that he was literally coming face to face with the reality that people do change over time. Sometimes the change was for the better, but then sometimes...

Ezell watched as Janice drove away, carrying two of the Richmond family's legacies. He turned to the door and took a deep breath before knocking. He recognized the feeling of apprehension that came over him at that moment, the same feeling from just before he took a seat at the counter. He laughed, thinking of all the spectators' reactions as they thought the boys were playing a prank. No, it was the real deal, just as that moment when the door opened.

# Chapter Twenty-one:
# The Awakening

David did not look shocked at all to see Ezell standing there. It seemed as if he had been at work all day and just wanted to sleep. It made sense, since Ezell's father made it known that parenting was in fact a full-time job. "What's up, David?" Ezell whimpered.

David looked Ezell up and down. "I thought you were in D.C.?" he said, uninterestedly.

*So, he has been staying updated.*

"I'm just home to visit," Ezell replied. "I thought I'd stop by and see you, if that's alright."

David stepped away from the door as if he was leaving the decision up to Ezell. He had made it all the way to the kitchen by the time Ezell decided to cross the threshold. "How's the family doing?"

Ezell closed the door behind himself and turned to examine the living room. There were toys everywhere, which he took no issue with. But what he found more repugnant were the liquor bottles and cigarettes laying around in plain sight. Unfolded clothes and unwashed laundry piled up into corners and atop furniture. It was as if no one lived at the house on a regular basis, and this was far left field for David, who was known for being well put together in many areas of his life, including cleanliness. Ezell was so muddled by the home's condition he almost forgot to respond to the question.

"My family is fine," he said, "at least I believe *most* of them are."

David ignored the subliminal message. He would not give Ezell the satisfaction of knowing he was aware that so many people were concerned about his well-being. He poured a glass of alcohol. "You want one?" he offered, holding the glass up.

Ezell had been staring at all the trophies and awards on the shelf in the living room. There were dozens of them, from "Athlete of the Year" to "Most Valuable Player" in several different sports. Then of course, the plaque for North Carolina's 1959 high jump champ, a record that had yet to be broken after four years. He turned to face David and shook his head, declining the drink. "No, I'm alright."

David came from the kitchen, moving clothes from a chair across from a recliner so Ezell could sit down. "You sure about that?" he asked. "You seem really stressed out."

That must have been a joke. It was too bad Ezell was not there for satire diversions from what was important. David was in the recliner, so Ezell sat before him, going off the script he had practiced in his head beforehand. "I know it's been a while since you heard from me, but during the last few months at A&T, I was constantly trying to see how you were doing, but I could never get up with you. You wouldn't return any of my calls, so I just stopped trying."

David shrugged. "I haven't had much time to be on the phone." He began drinking from the glass, content with the brief explanation he had given. Ezell felt they were already off to a bad start but continued anyway.

"You didn't forget about the pact we made, did you?" Ezell asked. "Remember when we said we would go after everything we wanted in life, no matter what? What happened to that?"

David had an apathetic look in his eyes while he stared into space. "I'm not the same person I was back then, E.Z., when are you gonna understand that?" he said.

"Maybe right now you're not feeling like yourself, and that's alright, you're human," Ezell said. "But don't give up just yet."

David sighed. "E.Z., won't you give it a rest already," he said, placing the empty glass down on the table next to him. "Those days are long gone. It's time for you to see reality for what it is. I was never who anyone thought I was, even you."

Ezell sat up in the chair, feeling the tension growing. "What do you mean?" he said. "You're David Richmond, the guy who can do anything."

David almost laughed at the comment, placing his arms behind his head to relax. "You sound ridiculous, E.Z.," he said, "I don't think you get what's actually going on."

Ezell was defensive. "Just hear me out, Hoppergrass."

"Don't call me that!"

Now David was staring Ezell straight in the eyes, something he had avoided doing the entire conversation. It was time to switch gears if Ezell wanted to have an effective intervention. Before he could regroup, David had taken his glass back to the kitchen. "You don't understand what it feels like having to live up to everyone's expectations," he said, filling the glass up to its brim. "Imagine having the entire city watching you your whole life, and once you make a mistake there's no coming back from it. It's even worse now, because the whole world is watching!"

Ezell concurred. "That's what I meant when I said I understand you, David," he said. "These protests have brought a lot of attention to the South, and those four little girls paid the price. Do you know they're still trying to find the guys who did it?"

David shook his head in disbelief at Ezell's naivety. "You think they don't know who did it, E.Z.? I wouldn't be surprised if it was the police themselves," he replied. "I swear, sometimes I feel like you live in a fantasy world where things only make sense to you."

That was the last straw for Ezell, who stood up to meet David as he came back into the living room. "Well, at least I'm doing the best I can with myself, David!" He said. "Look at you! Can you honestly say you're satisfied with where you are in life? I don't care if you don't believe you were ever as great as anyone thought, but *this* isn't who you are either, and you know it!"

"And why exactly does that matter to you?" David retorted. "Your life ain't in Greensboro no more, so stop worrying about what I do!"

Then everything began to make sense for Ezell. It must have been difficult for David to watch his friends graduate and move on with their lives with no restrictions, no marriages or children keeping them from going as they pleased. Not that David felt his children were a burden, because it was known that he loved Chip and Lynn and considered them the greatest blessings that came during his downward spiral. He was not jealous of his friends either, but like all human beings, he wanted better for himself. Sadly, he had convinced himself that *better* was unattainable.

David had sat down in the recliner again, breathing a bit heavier after releasing emotions he had clearly bottled up for a long time. Ezell sat down again after the atmosphere settled. He did not want to allow anger to misconstrue his message. "You know I went and heard Dr. King speak last month at the March on Washington," Ezell said. "He spoke about his dream not only for America, but for the world as well. Aren't you glad that being part of the movement makes us part of that dream?"

David sat quietly for a moment, staring directly past Ezell. His silence indicated that he had already thought deeply into the matter. "You ever thought about what it's gonna cost to make that dream happen?" he asked. "Our own lives haven't been the same after what we did, so you know this *dream* won't come without a cost. You see, the truth is that we're a bunch of walking targets, E.Z. Whether we're in the movement or not, they still hate us."

Ezell was taken back by the chilling response. David was never an individual who spoke idly, but sometimes his realism was appalling. Ezell took another breath. He felt that he had overstayed his visit but knew there were brighter times to reflect on that, in his opinion, outweighed the circumstances present that day. It was time to be completely candid if Ezell truly wanted to get through to his friend.

"David, I never told you this, but I've looked up to you since we met as kids," Ezell said. "You were always good at everything you did, and before you, the only hero I'd wanted to be like was Superman. But now you're not just a hero, you're my brother. It's just like it was when we ran track. I'm always on the sidelines rooting for you."

David shook his head. "You've always had too much faith in me, E.Z.," he said, "I ain't ever been anybody's hero."

Ezell held out his fist. "But we said we wouldn't stop until we changed the world," he said. "Remember? Let's do it."

David did not acknowledge the gesture, continuing to stare in oblivion. "Ain't nothing else I can do," he said.

Ezell felt a sharp pain go through his chest, something he had not felt in years. He put his hand down quietly, looking away from David, likely to hide the agony in his eyes. "Alright," he murmured before standing to his feet. "Well, I hope to see you around when I come back home. Job corps found me some work up in the mountains, so if you ever need me for..."

David was no longer invested in the conversation. "See you later, E.Z.," he said, quietly.

Ezell had accepted defeat before—many times, actually—but this was a loss he would never recover from.

He was sure of it. He knew David was still his brother, but there was nothing Ezell could do to pull him from the state he was in. If only there was enough time to keep trying, but there was not. Ezell had worked hard to get where he was, and he was determined to see how far he would go.

Though life had taken another unexpected turn, he refocused and continued to move forward.

## Chapter Twenty-two:
## Vows of the Unheard

Ezell picked through his growing afro in the mirror. During the late sixties, African Americans were embracing the concept of wearing their natural hair after decades of greasing it down or having it permed. It had been four years since Ezell left Howard University due to his skin condition's worsening. Sometime after, he was offered a position as a salesperson in New Bedford, Massachusetts. He had finally made it up North after all those years of wondering what life was like there. He loved his new job and all the friends he made while living in the city. There was one woman who had caught his eye a few months prior, and he was on his way to meet with her over dinner.

*

Ironically, Ezell had met Lorraine at a lunch counter one day on his way to work. She was from Chicago, Illinois and arguably one of the most beautiful women in New Bedford. Ezell did not want to rush things with her because he was genuinely interested in seeing where things would go if he let the relationship unfold at its own pace. But it turned out to be Lorraine who was impulsive and strong-willed.

"So, you're saying you would marry me?" she said boldly. "I'd marry me too. I'm a catch. My daddy thinks I'm too hard to deal with, but what does he know anyway?"

Ezell tried to reply. "Well see—"

"And just what is it with men and their egos? Lorraine continued. "Why do y'all always think you have to save everybody? Like you and your friends. I could've done that protest all by myself. I've never needed a man for anything."

Ezell chuckled. "Lorraine, you've never had to protest for anything," he said. "You grew up in a mostly integrated city. Besides, you don't know what you would do in a situation like that."

Lorraine disagreed. "I'm not scared of anything," she replied. "Or anybody. I do what I want, Mr. Blair."

Ezell did not respond. He thought the girl was adorable while trying to prove her strength, and secretly, her worth. Lorraine was a different type of girl, who tried to hide her true feelings behind heavy-handed, self-deprecating comments about herself when in reality, she was thoroughly invested in the guy who was brave enough to reignite an entire movement. "So, when are you gonna meet my dad?" she asked.

Ezell looked away for a moment. "I don't know—"

"Better yet, when will I meet your dad or the rest of your family?" Lorraine asked. "I want to visit North Carolina. I love the South. Ya know most of my family is from New Orleans."

"Yes, you told me."

Lorraine began stirring the curry in her bowl. "You may think we've got it made up North," she said, "but Southern food is the best. One day I'll make gumbo for you, okay?"

Ezell had never recalled gushing over any woman before. Likely because no woman had ever planned a future with him. He looked away from Lorraine to hide his affection, stirring the curry in his bowl. The moment was like the scene from *Lady and the Tramp,* just without the spaghetti and, well, the dogs, but the magic, the chemistry, and the innocent romance were there.

*

Ezell sat at the desk, nervously, his right knee shaking uncontrollably as he stared at all the paperwork before him. Lin, one of his coworkers, entered the room, spotting Ezell's anxiety almost immediately. "You alright, Ezell?" he asked.

Ezell sat up in the chair. "I'm okay, I've got everything done."

The man poured himself a cup of coffee. "Yeah, you've been getting your work done really fast the last few weeks," he said. "Is something bothering you?"

"No, I'm alright," Ezell replied, quietly.

"It's about Lorraine, isn't it?" Lin replied.

"She wants me to meet her dad!" Ezell exclaimed, "But I'm not ready to. Why do men have to meet their women's fathers anyway? Can't we just skip straight to the proposal?"

Lin laughed, sitting down at his desk. "That's not traditional, Ezell."

"Ah, who needs tradition anyway?" Ezell said. "I've never been a guy who followed the rules."

Lin was looking through a stack of newspapers. *Thousands Headed Down to Selma, Alabama in Wake of March* was one of the headlines he examined in the pile before coming across a paper on the sit-ins of Greensboro. "How are your friends doing now?" he asked. "The ones you started the protests with."

Ezell was pouring himself a cup of coffee now, as if he had ever needed an energy boost from another source. "Franklin lives in Charlotte, North Carolina with his wife and children. Joseph is in the military, and David... I'm actually not too sure what he's up to."

Lin placed the newspapers down. "I hear people aren't too happy now that the voting rights act has been passed," he said. "I don't think anyone was expecting the movement to progress the way it has, but we've come a long way in the last few years. You and your friends did a good deed for us."

Ezell was not sure how to accept the compliment. So much had occurred during the movement, so many tragedies.

Medgar Evers, an activist and secretary in Mississippi's branch of the NAACP, was murdered right in his driveway just hours after the televised civil rights address of President Kennedy. The former U.S president had openly expressed his concern of discrimination and made it clear he would do everything in his power to obliterate racial inequality. He managed to integrate a university in Alabama and was making attempts to integrate the high schools in the state as well.

Carole Robertson was a victim of the 16th Street Baptist Church bombing, and she had been selected to be one of the first African American students to attend an all-white school before she was brutally murdered along with Addie Mae Collins, Denise McNair, and Cynthia Wesley.

President Kennedy was assassinated just months after the bombing in November of 1963. He was the most recent president to be killed during his term. Two years after his murder, thousands of American citizens of many races marched from Selma to Montgomery, Alabama to protest black Americans being blocked from voting. One of the demonstrations was almost deadly on March 7th, 1965, and the event became known as Bloody Sunday. Once again, the tradition of the Jim Crow South was televised for the world to see, and this led to the passing of the Voting Rights Act of 1965.

The race war had risen to an all-time high, but through it all, effective change was happening. Ezell was still strictly grieved by all who had lost their lives in this fight. It was almost as if he suffered from survivor's guilt. How had he managed to make it out of that dime store alive that day? The turbulent occurrences of the civil rights movement were a constant reminder that life was fragile. If you truly loved someone, you had to let them know. Tomorrow is promised to no one.

\*

"And what makes you think you're good enough to have my daughter?" Lorraine's father demanded. "You ain't big as nothing, so how you gon' protect her?"

Ezell's teeth chattered. He stood next to Lorraine before her parents in their living room, fearing for his life. "Sir, I promise I won't let anything happen to her," he stuttered. "I'll do everything in my power to take care of her."

Lorraine stepped in front of her father. "Daddy, do you even know who you're talking to?" she asked. "Ezell is one of the reasons black Americans are transforming the South, so could you have a little more respect, please?"

"Lori, I don't give a damn who he is," the man replied, "I'm the reason you're alive, so whoever I say is fit to marry you is who you're gonna marry!"

Lorraine's face reddened. "And just what makes you think you have the right?" she snapped.

Ezell tried to calm her. "Baby, don't—"

"Ezell is asking you for my hand in marriage," she continued, "but I'm *telling* you that he's the man I'm gonna marry!"

Lorraine took Ezell by the hand. "Now, have I made myself clear?" she said, more calmly than before. "I love you, Daddy, but it's time for another man to take care of me, and I don't want anyone else but E.Z."

Her father was amused. "E.Z.?"

Ezell nodded. "It's my nickname. It's short for... never mind, sorry."

Lorraine's father sat next to her mother on the sofa. His daughter was resting her head on Ezell's shoulder, her fingers still interlocked with his. "Well?" Lorraine's mother said.

The older man took a deep breath. "Just how much is this wedding gon' cost?"

Lorraine squealed with joy, running to hug her father. "I knew you'd come through!" she yelled.

"If you're happy, I'm happy," her father said before glancing at Ezell. "But if you hurt my daughter, I got something back there for ya, and I don't miss."

Ezell could have fainted in relief. He had done it. He'd proposed and was getting married. What was remarkable about Lorraine was how she stood her ground against her father during a time when women knew better than to challenge the authority of men. That was the kind of woman Ezell wanted in his corner, and that was who he was prepared to start a new life with.

And so, they did.

# Chapter Twenty-three:
# Memories

Ezell and Lorraine had invited a few of their coworkers and friends over to their apartment for a special occasion. Ezell was celebrating his twenty-sixth birthday. "Man, just four more years til' thirty," he laughed.

"You're gettin' up there," Lin said.

"Lin, aren't you pushing forty?" Ezell replied.

Lorraine was in the kitchen stirring a pot of gumbo. "You all just sit right fine, the gumbo will be ready in just a minute, and I used my grandmother's secret recipe."

A few of her friends stood and watched as she prepared the food. "So, how do you like being married?" one of them asked. "Your family swore you were hell to deal with, now look at you."

Lorraine laughed. "I'm still hell to deal with, but I love it," she said. "I love him, but as much as I'd like for him to adapt here quicker, I know he misses home."

Ezell sat on the sofa with a glass of liquor cradled in his hands. He had unintentionally isolated himself from the guests, now staring blankly at whatever was in front of him while his mind was elsewhere. There was truth to what Lorraine said. Though Ezell had always wanted to venture out of his comfort zone and live in another city, he never thought he would feel so disconnected from the loved ones in Greensboro. He wondered if there would ever be a time when Franklin, David, Joseph, and himself would come together again to laugh and joke around, like he was trying to do with everyone present that night. Most importantly, Ezell wanted to reminisce on all the good memories with his friends, because after all the tragedies of the movement, it had become apparent that, one day, memories would be all he had.

His emotions had taken a sharp turn downward. He had an eerie feeling the entire night that he couldn't shake. Something was not right; he just couldn't point directly to it. He had noticed Lorraine laughing with some of the men who waited around the kitchen, but he wouldn't address it right then. Even if she felt there was nothing to address, he would call her out on it. Ezell had become unbearably territorial since he and Lorraine tied the knot. Though he was not a proclaimed fighter by any means, he would do what he felt was necessary to remind everyone that Lorraine *Blair* was his wife.

Lorraine answered the ringing phone in the kitchen. Her friends watched as her face slowly transitioned from cheerfulness to an expression of despair. "I'm so sorry," she said. "Yes, I'll go get him."

She placed the phone on the counter and took a deep breath.

"Everything alright?" one of the guests said.

Lorraine shook her head before walking to the living room. "Baby, would you answer the phone in the bedroom, please?"

Ezell stood from the couch. "Who is it?" he asked. "I'm not in the best mood to talk."

Lorraine walked to him, taking the drink from his hand. "You have to," she said quietly. "It's your mother."

Ezell's eyes went dull. *What exactly could be going on?* His mother would never call that late at night unless it was something she felt he needed to know immediately, and most times it was not good news. That dark feeling he had made sense now, but when he went into the bedroom and picked up the phone, he was not prepared for what his mother had to tell him.

\*

It turned out Ezell would have to make a trip back home anyway. He would have a few days to reconnect with his loved ones and reminisce on the good days as he'd wanted to, the only problem was that now his grandmother would no longer be there. One unfortunate thing for so many goal-driven people was that they could become so focused on their futures they forgot that many of their loved ones were growing old. Adelia had lived a long life, and Ezell could honestly say that because she was part of his, he was able to do the unthinkable. Now he would have to find a way to move on without his first best friend.

Many family friends stopped by to visit the Blairs during their time of bereavement. Corine kept herself busy, making sure the house was in order and cleaned from top to bottom. Lorraine worked alongside her mother-in-law to give Sheila and Jean breaks when they needed one. Ezell realized he had not seen his father for most of the day. Of course, he was taking the death of his mother hard, and he refused to show anyone the toll it was taking on him.

*

When the night came, Ezell lay next to Lorraine in his bed. She was holding his Jerry Mahoney puppet. Earlier that day he'd told her of his childhood dream to be a ventriloquist. She knew her husband loved music but was shocked to learn from her sister-in-law that he was a singer as well. "E.Z., you're just full of surprises, aren't ya?" she said before they went to bed. He was laying there, staring at the ceiling in complete darkness when he heard the front door open slowly.

*Who the--*

Ezell crept through the living room quietly, but no one was there. He lifted the window blinds and saw his father sitting on the steps of the porch. That must have been what the grieving man had been waiting for—to be alone, so no one could see his pain. He needed time to process the entire situation himself, so Ezell went outside to join him.

Ezell Sr. looked up at his son. "Junior, I'm happy you made it down here, son."

Ezell sat next to his father. Even through the shadowy area, he could see the man's eyes had swollen up. It was a surreal sight, to say the least. "Yeah, Dad, I'm home," he said. "I hope you're doing a little better."

Ezell Sr. looked up at the sky. "You know when I was a boy, your grandmother would sit with me under the stars, and I would always wonder what lies beyond that ginormous, dark wall."

Ezell nodded. "Me too."

Ezell Sr. turned to face his son. "Junior, I know I wasn't the best dad, and I was way harder on you than I should have been," he said. "I was so concerned about trying to teach you how to be a man because no one ever taught me, and I'm sorry for putting so much pressure on you."

Ezell looked away from him. That was the apology he had never wanted, simply because of how vulnerable it made him feel in that moment. He knew for certain his father had reached his lowest point and it hurt to see him that way, but he was grateful to know the man was human just like everyone else.

"Dad, there's no such thing as a perfect parent, but you tried your hardest and never gave up on your family, so I want to say thank you for always being there," Ezell said.

Ezell Sr. gazed at the stars again. "Your grandmother used to tell me that when there was a shooting star then something big was about to happen," he said. "Well, something big did happen, because having you as a son is a blessing I thank God for every day. I used to want you to carry on my legacy, but you've gone and made a legacy of your own. For years to come, people are gonna talk about what you and your friends did to change the world. But even aside from that, you're still my firstborn. You're *my* son."

Ezell was fighting back tears as a feeling of liberation came over him. "I love you, Dad."

"I love you too, Junior."

## Chapter Twenty-four:
## The Remaining Light

Ezell sat on the barstool. It had been a long week of work, and it was only Wednesday. It was not the job that stressed him out, but returning to reality after losing a loved one was ironically unrealistic. He had been to the bar every night, a habit that was already creating a wedge between him and his concerned wife. It was April 3rd, 1968, and many televisions were broadcasting a speech Dr. King was delivering at the men's sanitation strike in Memphis, Tennessee. Ezell would have watched the event from the bar but knew Lorraine wanted him home sooner than later. He placed a few bills on the counter and got down from the seat.

"Damn, for a little guy, you sure have a high tolerance," the bartender said. "I'm sure you'll be back tomorrow, huh?"

Ezell sighed. "If my wife don't kill me first, but we'll see."

*

Lorraine was seated at the kitchen table alone with a plate of half-eaten food before her and the trash can next to her. She stared at the television as Dr. King made his way to the podium to speak. Shortly after, Ezell entered quietly and locked eyes with his wife as he closed the door.

"Baby," he said.

"Your supper is in the fridge," Lorraine said sternly.

"I'm not hungry," Ezell replied, "I think I'll just go to bed,"

Lorraine nodded. "I take it you're still mourning," she said.

"And if so, what about it?" Ezell replied.

"What does it matter?" Lorraine said, getting up from the table, "You're never in your right mind to have a decent conversation, so don't even worry about it."

She walked into the living room to turn the television volume up and began folding the pile of clothes in a basket next to the couch. Ezell stared at the television screen for a moment as Dr. King spoke. In the speech, he addressed the threats he had received from unverified sources and assured the crowd and everyone watching that he was not fearful. Martin Luther King declared that he had been to the mountaintop and saw everything God had wanted him to see. When the speech was over, Ezell directed his attention to Lorraine again, who was clearly being passive aggressive, and this ticked him off to say the least.

"What's been going on with you?" Ezell asked. "You've been moody for the last month or so and overreacting to every little thing I do. Are you sure you're okay?"

Lorraine laughed in a sarcastic manner. "Well, if it isn't the pot calling the kettle black," she said. "I was gonna ask you the same thing."

Ezell followed Lorraine to the back of the kitchen where the washing machine was. "And what's that supposed to mean?"

Lorraine started a new load of clothes before turning to Ezell. "I know losing your grandmother was hard, just like I'm sure adapting to life up North is hard for you too," she said. "But, Ezell, I'm concerned about your mental state at this point. You running down to the bar to drink isn't gonna heal your insecurities."

Ezell backed away from Lorraine. "You think I'm insecure?"

Lorraine took a deep breath. "Ezell, you overreact to everything," she said. "We can never go out and have a good time, because God forbid another man even speak to me, you'll have a heart attack. Why are you so afraid I'm gonna leave you?"

"What reason do you have to stay?" Ezell demanded.

Lorraine winced. "What kind of question is that?" she exclaimed.

"One that I've been wanting to ask for a long time," Ezell said. "If I wasn't anyone important, would you have even given me the time of day? If I wasn't a leader in this movement, what would you find special about me?"

Lorraine rushed past Ezell for the sink. "Oh, please," she said, running water to wash the dishes. "It's just like my daddy said. We're thankful for what you've done for our people, but your activist title doesn't hold up the way you think it does in a marriage."

"That wasn't my point!" Ezell exclaimed. "Why me and no one else?!"

"Would you stop asking me that?!" Lorraine screamed. "If I wanted anyone else, do you think I'd be standing here arguing with you? Your self-esteem is so low you're steadily trying to force situations under your control, so you'll feel better about yourself!"

"That's not true."

"It is true!" Lorraine yelled. "You're so concerned about not being the man your father raised you to be that you've become just that!"

Ezell was furious now. Lorraine had hit the nail directly on its head, but he would not let up just yet. "No need to worry about my dad," he said, "worry about yours!"

"Excuse me?"

"Your dad was right," Ezell continued. "You would do yourself some good if you stopped speaking out of turn and just do what you're asked to like every other woman does! I'm a man! Instead of complaining, how bout you say thank you that I'm putting a roof over your head?"

It was the smoothest backhand Ezell had ever endured. He stood in silence as his face recovered from the strike his wife had bestowed upon him. Lorraine stared him in the eyes as the moment simmered down to a state of airlessness. No words were being said, but the tension could have been read like a book.

"I don't know what your definition of a *man* is, but it won't do in this house," Lorraine said assertively. "I never asked you to be anyone other than yourself, but you're so blinded by your past that you can't even see that. So what if you're not the biggest and strongest guy I know? So what? That wouldn't make you a *man* anyway."

She took Ezell by the hands. "But who you are is an individual who learned to bounce back when life knocks you down, someone who can do anything. But until you look into the mirror and face yourself, and your demons, you'll never find whatever it is you're looking for in this life." Lorraine kissed Ezell on the lips before heading down the hallway. Ezell sat down at the table, examining the sitting food and the trash can. He threw the food away, placed the dishes in the sink, and gathered the rest of the trash in the apartment.

\*

The walk back from the neighborhood dumpster was like a therapy session. Only Ezell would have to counsel himself, while intoxicated, and finally ask the lingering questions. *What am I most afraid of?* He already knew the answer. Ezell had a fear of abandonment from the day he realized many situations were, in fact, out of his control. Starting with his father going off to war, his bandmates exiling him, his first love leaving him behind in Greensboro, and, of course, the memories of all his failed attempts to save David from depression haunted him the most. His grandmother's death was the last straw. Death was irreversible, so there was no way he could alter reality any longer.

Ezell staggered onto the steps of the porch, glancing up at the stars. Nothing was happening, but there was a calmness that filled the night. It was as if the dust had finally settled, and Ezell came to terms with the fact that he did not always have to be optimistic. Sometimes he was not doing well, and he did not have to pretend to be, because the reality was that the world was unpredictable and terrifying at times. He loved his wife and wanted to be the man she deserved, and the man he aspired to be like was himself, even if he wasn't sure exactly who that was yet. He got up and walked back into the house as the moon shined down upon the city.

Ezell always loved the belief that where there was light, there was hope, and he still believed his troubles had not been in vain.

# Chapter Twenty-five:
# One Last Stand

Ezell came up the stairs of the building where he worked. He had slept well the night before. He slept on the couch, but he slept well, even so. He and Lorraine had made up that morning over breakfast, so the day was starting off well for him. The sun seemed to be shining brighter than it ever had, and the cool temperatures made being outdoors so pleasing. Ezell was in a great mood, so he was surprised to see many of his coworkers crying as he entered the office. It was also strange that not many workers were present that day.

Lin was counseling one of the sobbing employees by the main entrance when he saw Ezell come into the office. Ezell walked over to the man with a vibrant smile, though he was still baffled by the despondency happening around them. "How are ya, Lin? What's going on around here? I noticed the parking lot is practically empty."

Lin nodded. "Yeah, the GM is letting people go home," he replied. "Did you watch the news this morning?"

Ezell shook his head. "No, I didn't have time," he said, "what did I miss?"

Lin paused for a moment. "Well, you know Dr. King spoke in Memphis a couple nights ago at the sanitation strike. There'd been a bunch of threats on him for a while, but last night when he got back to his hotel, they..."

The man would not even finish the sentence. Ezell peered at him for a moment. "They what?" he asked.

Lin shook his head. "They killed him, Ezell."

The coworker may as well have been speaking a foreign language, because Ezell was having a hard time processing what he was told. "What do you mean they killed him?" he asked. "Dr. King can't *die*."

Lin did not respond, prompting Ezell to look around at his weeping coworkers still present in the building. It was clear that many of them were in too much shock to move from their seats. Ezell turned back to Lin. "Dr. King can't die, can he? He would never let that happen, so what are you talking about?"

Lin placed his hand on Ezell's shoulder. "It was out of his control, Ezell, just like it's out of ours."

Ezell took a deep breath, then he did the best smile he could. "Well, I guess he warned us," he said. "He was trying to tell us his time was near, but who would've thought..."

Lin nodded. "We've come a long way, haven't we?" he said. "We'll keep moving forward. We owe it to him."

Ezell sighed. "So, what about today?"

"Just go on back home. I know you want to be with Lorraine anyway," Lin said.

"I'm always ready to spend a day with my baby," Ezell replied.

The two men laughed. That was what they needed before the silence returned. Lin sighed. "In his own words, 'This too shall pass,'" he said.

Lin headed down the hallway as Ezell stood in silence.

\*

Once he was outside, Ezell could feel the heat settling in. The passing clouds had cast a shadow upon him, but when they were gone, Ezell turned to face the sun, and it was still shining brighter than he could ever recall. It was still supposed to represent the beginning of a new era, but the world would have to be willing to leave the old one behind.

Many news reporters asked that citizens of the United States mourn silently and to express their sentiments of Dr. King's death in the way he lived his own life, through peaceful, nonviolent demonstrations. Unfortunately, that would not be the case, as many enraged Americans took their anger directly to the streets through a series of riots that left several cities in the country in partial ruins. They had lost their leader—no, they'd had their leader taken from them—and someone would pay the price for it, even if the entire nation went up in flames. If there was no justice, then there was no peace.

And among all the chaos that broke loose, especially in the South, there was a mourning that encompassed the entire nation. It was like the cry from the story in the bible when Moses warned Pharaoh that there would be a weeping like no other just before the angel of death descended upon Egypt. People of all races were disheartened to learn the news of such an exemplary leader who had brought his race so far and was taken down before his vision came to fruition. Schools were dismissing their grieving students and employers were releasing their workers. The tragic loss was nearly unbearable, and all of Dr. King's followers had one question in mind—

*Where do we go from here?*

\*

Lorraine came up the stairs of the apartment to find the door cracked open. She was hesitant to enter, fearing that someone had broken into her home, but she heard sniffling from the kitchen. Ezell's fedora hat and car keys were laying on the counter. She barged into the home, yelling for her husband. "Ezell, what's going on? Where are you?!"

Lorraine found the man leaning against the wall on the kitchen floor. She crouched down next to him, shrieking while bending to his side. "Baby, are you okay?"

Ezell's eyes were swollen as if he had been crying all day long, because he had been. There was no point in waiting for an answer. Lorraine took Ezell by the hand and sat next to him. "It's a terrible thing that they've done," she said softly. "He didn't deserve it. Dr. King was one person I feel should have lived a long time. At least long enough to see everything he worked for pay off."

Ezell wiped his falling tears. "Just watching him on the television the other day, and seeing him step away from the podium," he whimpered, "it's like he knew he was about to leave us. I felt it coming but never believed it would actually happen, because who would want to hurt someone like him? I thought Dr. King would see us the whole way through."

Lorraine tightened her grip on Ezell's hand. This was the most vulnerable she had ever seen her husband, and it was painful to watch. She smiled. "Here's something I think you'd like to hear," she said. "You came in a little late while he was speaking, so you missed one part when he discussed how he was stabbed in the chest by some demented woman a long time ago. Do you remember that?"

Ezell nodded. "Yeah, I do."

Lorraine continued. "Well, the blade came so close to his heart that the doctor said had he even sneezed, he would have died. A little white girl wrote him a letter and said she was happy he didn't sneeze. He said he was happy he didn't as well, because he wouldn't have been around in 1960 when students all over the South started doing sit-ins. You hear that, Ezell? He thought about you all during his last speech. What you did was really special to him."

Ezell sniffled again. "I'm nobody's hero, and I'm nowhere as great as Dr. King," he said. "I just wonder if his children will ever know how amazing their father was."

Lorraine sat quietly for a moment before placing Ezell's hand on her stomach. "I wonder the same thing about our children," she said, quietly.

Ezell stared at his wife, who was not sure if she should smile or cry, so she did both. He rubbed his hand across her stomach until he felt a spot that was a bit warmer than anywhere else. There was a kick, and Ezell felt his own heart skip a beat. The life inside of his wife's stomach was what he'd helped create, which meant some months from then, he would be a father. It was a lot to process in the moment, but it was by far his proudest moment. He kissed Lorraine on the lips before laying in her lap.

"I'll do my best," he said, calmly. "I never break my promises."

# Chapter Twenty-six:
# Triumph in Defeat

After Dr. King's death, every public school and business was integrated on a national level. The impact of the tragedy left no more room for discussion on the issue of racial inequality. The civil rights movement came to an end after twelve long years of activism. The victory was a historical milestone and landmark for the United States, but it was also bittersweet because of everything and everyone lost along the way. The world had now entered a new era. Ezell was now the father of three children who would never know a life separated by color lines. They would, however, be avid fans of their father's puppet shows.

Two of the children sat on the bed as Ezell held the Jerry Mahoney puppet in his lap. "Say, Jerry, have you heard of Superman?" he said. "Why of course, I know all about Superman! What about you, kids?"

"Tell us!" his son and daughter said. "Tell us about Superman!"

Ezell smiled. "Well, if you haven't heard about the greatest hero of all time, he's faster than a speeding bullet!"

His daughter's mouth went agape. "Woah!"

Ezell continued. "He's more powerful than a locomotive," he raised the puppet into the air swiftly, "and he can leap tall buildings with one single bound."

"Like Uncle David!" his son said.

Ezell paused for a moment. "Yeah, just like your Uncle David," he said. He got up and sat between his two children, pulling them into a hug. "And he's big and strong just like your Uncle Frank, and smart and witty just like Uncle JoJo."

Lorraine had been standing by the door for several moments before she finally entered the room, carrying their youngest daughter with her. "And Superman is handsome, and brave, with a heart only half the size of your amazing dad's," she said, sitting down next to her family on the bed.

Ezell laughed. "But he'll never be lucky enough to find a woman as beautiful as your mother," he said.

His daughter was curious. "Does Superman ever die?" she asked.

The question caught everyone off guard, but her brother somehow had an answer prepared. "Duh, he has to die!"

The little girl was in denial. "Why so?!" she retorted. "He's a hero, so how can he save the world if he dies?"

Ezell and Lorraine laughed at their children's feud. It was an every night thing that always helped them unwind for bed.

"He's a hero, so he has to die so he *can* save the world, duh!" the boy said.

Ezell paused in astonishment. His son's words resonated with him so much it felt as if time was standing still. *A hero has to die?* Where had he learned that message? The boy didn't seem to think much of what he'd said and had begun playing with the puppet along with his sister.

*Well, out of the mouth of babes.*

*

The children were in their beds sleeping soundly. Ezell smiled at them before closing the door, quietly. He carried a scrapbook into the kitchen where Lorraine was cleaning and sat down at the table. "You gonna be up all night going down memory lane?" she asked.

"No, I just wanted to see how far I've come now that we're in our new home. It's been a long journey, wouldn't you say?"

Lorraine nodded. "Yes, it has."

Ezell examined photos of his high school and college graduations, his first day on the job in New Bedford, and all sorts of childhood photos his mother had given him the last time he was home.

Lorraine came to his side, placing her arms around his back. They were looking at a picture of Ezell riding a tricycle as a toddler. "Who would've imagined who that little boy would have grown up to be," she said gently. "You've definitely given our children something to live up to."

Ezell smiled. "I want them to find their own path, the same way I did," he said. "It's funny, as parents we're their first teachers, but I'm learning so much from them as well."

Lorraine could have shed tears of joy. "So, you think you've found it now?" she asked. "You've found what it is you're supposed to learn in your life?"

Ezell nodded. "Yes," he said, "I can finally say I have." He glanced down to see the family portrait he had taken with his wife and children just a few months earlier and his heart throbbed to see the gleeful smiles on everyone's faces.

"And I'm blessed to know that if I don't achieve anything else in this life, I've made one beautiful family," he said with tears in his eyes. "*We* made one."

Ezell kissed his wife before shutting the scrapbook, closing the biggest chapter of his life.

What David said had been true. Now that Ezell was a parent he understood life in a deeper sense, and now he understood that a man, a hero, was someone who was willing to give up their life for what they believed in. Perhaps he had been introduced to this lesson a long time before when he sat down at the lunch counter with his friends. They knew the costs, and their lives were one of them, but everything was worth it if it meant changing the lives of others. That was the ultimate price Dr. King had paid, and he made it clear in his final moments that he was prepared to give his life for his people to be free. Ezell realized that the concept of risking your life for others was so much easier to embrace now that he had something of his own to protect—his family.

And now, he could finally say he had become a man.

# Chapter Twenty-seven:
# The Legacy Continues

The world had been recovering from a global pandemic that lasted longer than anyone had likely expected it to. However, that did not stop Ezell from taking safety precautions while going out in public. It was common knowledge that the elderly was at high risk of catching the virus that had affected so many people. His granddaughter, Raquel, was relentless in asking him if they could go to the park after her homework was finished. She knew in her family that education came first, so when the work was completed, they took a trip down to a local park.

Ezell wore his mask in case he had to interact with any people at the location. "Come on, Grandad!" Raquel said, standing at the park's entrance. "The sun will be down by the time you make it to the gate."

Ezell paced himself, using his cane to keep himself steady. "Raquel, don't let this stick fool ya, I'll take you on in a foot race any day. Believe me, I'm pretty fast."

Raquel laughed. "Whatever, slowpoke," she said before noticing the plaque on the gate. *Dr. Jibreel A. Khazan Park.* "Granddad, why did they name the park after you?" she asked.

Ezell shrugged. "I'm gettin' old," he said, "old people get nice things done for them sometimes."

Ezell had legally changed his name decades earlier to Jibreel Khazan after joining an Islamic center. However, his granddaughter was too young to know much about his life before he embraced the religion. Most kids didn't think much of their grandparents' first names anyway. Ezell sat on the bench as Raquel played with a few of her friends from school who had come to the park as well. Next to him were some of the parents of the other children, who were inquisitive after learning the park was named after Ezell. One of Raquel's friends had likely spread the news.

"So, you grew up in the South?" one of them asked. "Life is still much different down there, I'd assume."

One of the fathers sighed. "Life is different everywhere now that we're coming out of a pandemic," he said. "It's like children are learning how to interact with each other again after being isolated from one another for so long."

Ezell concurred. "I've watched the world undergo much change throughout my life," he said, "and it's still changing."

The other adults smiled. "Well, from the looks of that plaque on the gate, you were a big part of that change," one of them said.

Ezell smiled while watching all the children of different races playing together, pushing each other on the swings, chasing each other around in the grass, unaware that there was ever a time when their physical appearance would have made all the difference in just wanting to have fun. "People might actually learn to coexist with one another" he said, "because I believe this next generation is gonna get it right."

A little while later, the parents were calling for their children. Raquel and her classmates were preparing for a project they had in history class to celebrate Black History Month. They were only in the fourth grade, and no one had ever taught them much about the Underground Railroad or the Montgomery bus boycotts. Raquel had never even heard of the event she was assigned to research.

The children said farewell to one another, and the adults did the same to Ezell. "What was your name again, sir?" one of the parents asked.

"I'm Jibreel Khazan," Ezell said, "but you can call me E.Z."

Ezell turned to face the sun. It was high in the sky serving as the guiding light it had always been, leading people onto the path they were meant to take if their hearts were open to listen. He no longer envisioned the coming of a new age, now he could feel it.

Raquel had opened her history book to the page she placed a bookmark at. It was the lesson on the Greensboro Four, a group of students from North Carolina Agricultural and Technical University. They were credited with starting a series of protests in North Carolina that spread to several other cities in the Southern United States. She examined the photo of the four men coming out of a store. One of the two who were looking at the camera seemed familiar, so she took the book to where her grandad was, sitting next to him on the bench.

"You ready to go now?" Ezell asked.

Raquel stared at her grandad for a moment, then back at the guy in the book. "Yes, I'm ready to go," she said. "I have to start on my history project. It's due by the end of February."

Ezell nodded. "It's important that you know your history, Raquel, because if not, you'll repeat the same mistakes."

Raquel showed Ezell the picture of the Greensboro Four in the textbook. "Grandad, do you know anything about the sit-in movement?" she asked.

Ezell smiled.

This book is dedicated to the memories of David Richmond (1941-1990), Franklin McCain (1941-2014) and everyone who risked their lives in the battle for civil rights. Thank you for your diligence and sacrifice. Your work was not in vain.

"We left our footprints in the sands of time.
Now it's your turn."

-   Ezell Blair